COSMIC CAGE

Gay SF Erotica

JEAN-PAUL L. GARNIER
PETER SCHUTES

Cosmic Cage: Gay SF Erotica
Copyright © 2024 by Peter Schutes Publishing.
First Edition © 2024
All Rights Reserved.

ISBN: 978-1-963667-13-4

The story, all names, characters, and incidents portrayed in this production are fictitious. No identification with actual persons (living or deceased), places, buildings, and products is intended or should be inferred.

Cover Illustration by Oliver Benson

This book is for ADULT AUDIENCES ONLY. It contains substantial sexually explicit scenes with multiple partners and graphic language which may be considered offensive by some readers.

All sexual activity in this work is consensual and all sexually active characters are 18 years of age or older.

Two erotic SF tales of incarceration will keep you captivated and aroused.

IN EACH OTHER'S ARMS - I'm an Earthling, surrounded by other life forms, presumably male. We all live in a dreary prison with no windows somewhere off-planet. We have no memory of how we got here or why we're even here. The need for connection is intense; it often results in interspecies couplings that defy the imagination. I feel a bond with my fellow prisoners that only grows stronger as we find new and exciting ways to be intimate with one another. When will we ever break free from our bondage and see the light of day, any day, somewhere in the universe?

THE ORCHARDMAN - My name is Shepard Boone, and I'm a full-blooded Monachee. Until a plague rendered most of the planet sterile, we were just a bunch of Virginia hill folk who minded their own business. We were a little different, though. See, our menfolk can carry babies, too. As was tradition, my Pa put a baby in me, my firstborn son. Then came the great sickness. Our fertility was a prize that needed to be captured and harnessed for the propagation of the wealthy "helmsmen" who ruled over the decimated population. We're just chickens in a coop, popping out more chickens for the wealthy. Will we ever know freedom again?

CONTENTS

IN EACH OTHER'S ARMS

for Jean Genet

by Jean-Paul L. Garnier

Introduction: When Species Fuck

I'm dreaming of alien sex.

I'm dreaming of human sex, too, and the violence of it as proclaimed by theorists, the "erotic, death-bearing unconscious" that cannot stand (as Julie Kristeva reminds us) anything other than the lightest brush against the other.[*]

I am also dreaming of the reparative possibilities of sex on personhood, whereby the discrete categories of the familiar and the foreign are revealed to be one and the same: "The foreigner is within me, hence we are all foreigners."[†]

Science fiction has long imagined the meeting of human and non-human lives in a ideological spectrum that ranges from utopia, and euphoria, to dissolution and bio-death. The tentacled oankali of Octavia E. Butler's Xenogenesis trilogy drink human cancer cells, pheromonally altering the chemical composition of bodies and inserting themselves into tripartite relation-

---

[*] Kristeva, Julia. 2024. *Strangers to Ourselves*. Columbia University Press, p.192.
[†] Ibid.

that nest in an ambivalent area between rape and wish-fulfilment for the human characters. Psychic 'foxen' offer alluring body-mind bonds in Sherri S. Tepper's *Grass*. The human and non-human protagonists of Samuel R. Delany's novels inhabit positions of power and abjection alike in their sexualization; sex is at once central to his SF-nal world-building and important narrative tissue in connecting these fictional lives together. To fuck (or to not fuck) is to have a body—and to have a body, in this world or others, is always political.

Jean-Paul Garnier dedicates this volume to Jean Genet, and the invocation is an appropriate one for a work set in an enigmatic off-world penitentiary populated by a dazzling array of non-human lives, many of whom interact with the (human) main character in a series of beautifully-written sexual trysts that work to find solace—and even dignity—in a place of abjection. Genet himself, of course, wrote of his experiences in the Mettray Penal Colony in *Miracle of the Rose* (1946), within which he documents the homosocial society of which he became part. Hierarchies of mannerism (butch, femme), sensitivities of costume and gesture mark partners, antagonists, lovers. Powerplays organize the prison yard: who is physically larger? The savviest pimp? The most cunning guard-circumventer? Speaking of those: the mechanisms (and arbiters) of incarceration become an erotic force in their own right: an amorous 'third' as intrusive and irresistible as any oankali. Writing of another prisoner, Bulkaen, Genet expresses "I was drawn to him by the force of love, which was opposed by the force of supernatural but brawny creatures who kept me from going to him by fettering my wrists..."* The gaolers of Garnier's work maintain a strict rule: each night, the human protagonist shares his

---

* Genet, Jean. 2000. *Miracle of the Rose*. New York: Grove Press, p.24.

cell with another prisoner, but never with the same prisoner for consecutive nights.

The prisoners form an androcentric utopia, of sorts, finding ways to give and receive pleasure in the face of often radically different bodies and oppressive circumstances. Puddles, trees, lizards, crabs, telepaths ... all of them fuck. In this fucking is a beautifully rendered desire for return, for universality. Garnier's characters navigate connection through speech and touch and memory and the ever-present threat of violence and even death. Whether they succeed in finding liberation is for you, dear reader, to discover for yourself.

Donna Haraway speaks of "entanglements" as "contact zones" between species, asking us what, or *who*, exactly we are touching when we encounter another species.* The act is not necessarily erotic; it is political, ontological, and ethical. The prisoners of Garnier's In Each Other's Arms model a praxis of connection, extending such inquiry across a dazzling array of lifeforms. Garnier's writing, too, is political, ontological, and ethical. The line between guard and prisoner is, or becomes, diffuse, with a resolution that arguably redeems the sentient subject. To act violently, Garnier seems to suggest, is an act of imposition; to connect, to be embodied, and seek communion with other bodies, it its own panacea.

I invite you to meet these lives on the pages to come. Perhaps you will be revolted; perhaps you will be aroused. Perhaps you will embrace them with all the strength your arms can muster; perhaps you will recoil, anemone-quick.

I hope, either way, you dream.

Phoenix Alexander
    Riverside, California, 28th August, 2024

---

* Donna Haraway, *When Species Meet*.

IN EACH OTHER'S ARMS

The days were all wrong. They undulated from way too long to ever so brief. What kind of planetary tilt would cause that evolutionary fluke I could not say, but wherever we were it was all done with lighting which was too bright and of a sickly cast. Some of the species didn't seem to mind, while others winced and covered their eyes most of the time. I was among those who found it uncomfortable and would have given anything for a pair of shades, but nothing like that was to be found here. The thing with the eyes was a dead giveaway for who was who. The guards paid no mind to the lighting, and one could tell those adapted to darker planets by the need to tear a piece of the uniform and fashion it into a sort of blindfold with tiny slits to filter the ever harsh lights. This practice was forbidden by the guards and brought with it severe punishment, but the light sensitivity must have been worse because they'd be right back at it after having the fabric removed and subsequent thrashing. I was lucky to be somewhere in the middle of that spectrum, for I had felt the wrath of those prods the guards carried and wasn't eager to provoke them again.

The guards were always neutral, whether handing out a beating or herding us into the mess. Nothing seemed to alter their moods and it made us wonder if they were an organic species at all. Most inside the prison were, but despite all of the conjecture none of us knew a thing about our captors. Rumors abounded, and many claimed to know, but the stories contradicted one another and if one happened to ring true, some occurrence would smash the logic of it.

Whoever they were they governed by routine, one that was confusing and difficult to make sense of in the short scale, but the longer one resided here the more it would come into focus, hopefully. The structure was insane by human reasoning, but it was structure nonetheless. And one obediently followed it or paid heavy costs: from thrashings, to the hole, or worse yet – some of the labors that would be forced upon us. Cruelty is the same everywhere, but our captors had refined it into an artform. That is not to say that no pleasures were found here, but they certainly weren't provided by the guards. Those we found in each other's arms, though it wasn't always arms, I have to admit.

The food was bad, the water foul, the sleeping arrangements sordid, and the air even worse – but one makes due with what they have, or tries, at least. Some fared better than others, another indication of our differences and similarities. Those least affected we assumed were in some way related to the guards, either their creations, or their creators. Others were so debilitated that they were near catatonic. The latter could only be pitied as they were in such a sorry state as to be unable to convey even the most basic of needs, but some of us tried to comfort them anyway, even though we had no way of knowing if our efforts were even remotely successful. Still, we tried, together in our misery and the possible sharing of our pleasures, mammalian or otherwise.

In single file they led us down the narrow, brightly lit hallway toward the rec-room. The hallway had no windows and neither did the rec. As long as I'd been here I still hadn't seen one, nor had anyone I had spoken to. But with so many languages, and the possibility of different wings with completely different atmospheres, there was no way of knowing for sure. The hallway was long and barren with nothing to count but one's steps, each other, and the guards. The latter two always being the same, but not the steps, for some did not step nor use legs for locomotion, and often fatigue would get the best of a fellow inmate, and if he collapsed then he would be taken. Only then would our numbers change, and we would likely never see him again.

The guards did not seem to derive pleasure from these happenings; their expressions never altered whether removing a dead man, delving out punishment, or announcing meal time. Their narrow slits for mouths remained unchanged, slightly upturned as if about to smile, and menacing throughout. Whether they enjoyed their roles or not, one could not say, but their calm unwavering demeanor suggested that they were not bothered in the least by circumstance. They were also eerily silent. But when it came time to pass out discipline, or even just give out orders, they could be oppressively loud, nearly breaking one's eardrums. Just one more weapon in a barrage of techniques used to keep us in line.

But today the long walk to the rec was progressing without incident. I was looking down and counting steps, trying to adhere to the "no eye contact" rule, which was nearly impossible to maintain with eyes located just about everywhere on so many species. There was no reason not to allow us to look at each other, aside from making sure that no friendly glances would be exchanged. The rules, and the place, were designed so as to remove any possibility of comfort. But we would find our ways. With so much time on our appendages we would find a way, our small defiance in a world of suffering, for some of us the last reason for being. They could doom us, but they couldn't completely kill that which gave pleasure, or those things that the mind does to seek it. The guards might be unflappably even, but we were men, variable, as full of passion as the guards were devoid of it. For some, that very passion had driven them to commit the crimes that had begun their story of descent to this awful place. Many still had no idea why they had been sent here. I supposed that there were as many reasons as there were species, or no reason at all. The place could have been a galactic dumping ground for undesirables, a menagerie for some filthy rich mogul, or some sick experiment. No indication was ever given as to the prisoner's purpose, but a prison it certainly was. Some inmates freely confessed to crimes worthy of this place, others vehemently proclaimed their innocence, so in many ways it resembled any prison. But here there was something else going on, everyone could sense it. And it was written all over the cold, expressionless faces of the guards.

We entered the rec-room as the lights snapped on, full bright like noon in the desert. The room was nothing but a square with a circle painted on the floor. Every visit was the same, we were to walk around the circle in silence, for an hour, or whatever time interval it was, and then we would be allowed a brief moment, fifteen minutes or so, to sit down, converse or speak freely with each other, as long as there was no touching and no one raised their voices. Standing was also forbidden during these brief respites. For most, the conversation was welcome, at least when the group wasn't too full of language barriers or the silent types. Most of us that had been here a long time had found at least some way of communicating. Some species kept to themselves. I was in the former category and fortunately human vocal cords and limbs were capable of a wide enough variety of sound and gesture to make some alien languages possible to reproduce. Other species were not so lucky in their specificity.

With a signal from the guards we commenced our walk. Round and round, following the blue line on the slate gray floor, nothing changing but the circle of shadows that were nearly blotted out from the intensely bright lights. Some suffered through it, others took the opportunity to keep what was left of their strength. It was an easy way to tell how long someone had been in. But it didn't matter how you felt about it, you walked the circle or you were punished. So, we walked. I had long since passed being resentful that they made us circle so pointlessly, for this room was the biggest that I had ever seen in the prison, and the scant sense of open space was a small comfort, not much, but something. So, I circled, and I kept my head down and hoped that there would be no beatings for anyone, for if there was too much trouble, they could decide to skip the sitting and talking session, and this was the only time we were allowed to speak in groups. They kept us quiet in the mess, and at bunk time we were generally separated into pairs, occasionally a trio, but that was rare. Our bunkmates were different every time, some kind of ro-tation, presumably to keep everyone from plotting es-cape, and while this made group planning near impossible, it couldn't stop us from being someone's warmth in the cold. I suppose it was the same reason we were allowed no words in the mess. Our social time in the circle was too brief for much in the way of mean-ing, but our captors must have recognized some in-herent need to socialize and used it as a pressure valve of sorts.

And we walked and walked, and fortunately today no one fell or shouted or cried out for mercy, we just circled until the call came to sit and speak freely. When the call came you were to move within the circle, face one another, and sit where you were, no moving around, so you didn't get to choose who you sat with. In some way, I think this made us more tolerant and friendly with our fellow inmates, same as the bunk rotation. One couldn't rely on having a friend, but it had a positive effect on us as a group, for when you cannot have a friend you must learn to rely on strangers. So, when we sat, you made the man next to you a friend, no matter what sort of man he was, or if that was even relevant in his species.

Today I sat next to a man whose skin looked like bark, and on my other side, someone who resembled a puddle of bronze. The puddle, if he spoke, was in a language incomprehensible to me, so I turned to the bark man. His arms branched out in various directions and were graceful in their vegetable way, but he was no tree. Those limbs moved with rare rapidity and he must have been a formidable fighter when on the outside. It was difficult not to flinch when he gestured, but one got used to his speed, and his voice was gentle and low and lulled one away from the anxiety caused by his movement. I had spoken to his kind before, as there were several in my block, but there was something softer about him, perhaps he was younger, or older, I could not say. He extended his branching arm that terminated in a nest of lilting twigs and raised it in the air. I did the same with my hand. It was a formal greeting we all used in the circle, since touch was forbidden.

"Huught. The name you may call me. For the first time we sit." His voice was ever so gentle, like soft fur compared to the breaking glass shouts of the guards.

"Gerrold. I am pleased to be together now."

Since conversations with other inmates were uncommon outside of bunk time they were treated with a certain formality and respect. It could be years before you sat next to the same being again, this fleetingness of relationship gave those moments extra weight instead of the intended dehumanization, or whatever equivalent word in the multitude of languages and tongues.

Again, his rich bass came, "We circled well." He was referring to the exercise period passing without incident, without violence.

"Yes. I am glad to have met in peace. Watching a man hurt callouses one to new friends." It was a formal response, but one that expressed a broader caring. If one did not speak of friendship in the beginning of meeting it was typically driven by some inbuilt xenophobia, or physical revulsion to bodily differences. More often than not it came from newcomers. Those who had lived here long knew that it was only shapes loosely sketching an obscure outline of who a man was.

"Friend. New. Yes. Not easy with such false light, not the finest, but for a friend, for you..." his lovely voice drifted away but the twigs of his hand danced in rearrangement and ever so slowly, mesmerizingly, the smallest dollop of orange began to emerge there. In a world of gray it was the most beautiful thing I had ever seen. I would have given anything to touch it but instead cautiously leaned in as close as would be allowed without calling attention to the guards.

His arm remained in place, perfectly still as he bowed to look me in the eyes. "Look to the guards. When all have turned. The moment will pass quickly."

I did as he said and when the moment came brought my face to his hand, drawn by some shared instinct for fragrance. A puff of magenta dust came out in a near invisible plume and spiraled through the air between us as I breathed in, and it entered through my nose.

A thousand orgasms in spring exploded into my mind. Long dewy grasses undulated in silky winds. The sun on my back was a pleasing embrace. Root penetrated soil, deeper as it became more moist the further down it went. It grew from the inside out, blossoming new flesh as it expanded toward the life-giving stars. All those suns I had seen in my life, I had no idea... Each had lapped at me with a grace that skin alone could understand. Glory. As if a planetwide chorus erupted into the sky and into the core. Upwards and downwards at the same time. A vine which could reach the heavens.

Body slacked and tightened, reversing the process, then back again. Serenity of falling leaves. Each photon felt. Microscopic life-giving rain of light, full spectrum and complete with barbiturate-like killing of pain. Now grounded, now sailing on a breeze, nothing more than a mote. Each state exchanged places and worked together somehow. It was both, simultaneous, a dichotomy which seized my loins, gently bringing me to treetop heights, always toward the light. And if I'd fear a fall, it would ease me down in a slow back and forth, swaying cradle-like and peaceful.

A contentedness emanated from my partner. I could see him still in the gray room while I soared the skies above. He was a root, an anchor. My safe tether. His release had become mine, together in such different places, wondrous places so far away from prison walls. But it was not over, and I couldn't waste it on such thoughts. Huught softly reminded me, showed me clouds that blocked the sensuous light but poured equal relief as if ever so slightly touched by a thousand delicate hands. The slow drip of water filtering through soil burst every sense alive, a joining of elements, all but fire, but fire was the life inside, so all joined into a rapturous one.

A symbiosis... Then... What was left of me was an epiphyte clinging to Huught, but not taking. Occupying the same space but without give or take. An equilibrium, a balance. And while the scale would not tip, beauty – bright, shining and full of passion that had receded so far as to almost be forgotten. But now it rushed upon us in timeless ways. Swaddled us in the throes of something ancient, a ritual of dirt, which was not dirty, but rather mingled with those who had come before, all knowing in its neglect of confinement. To stay in one place did not mean to be stuck. All that which was good flooded, came to us, bathed us in the ancient ritual of unification.

And then the brittle voices of the guards. The room's four walls fell into place. The gentleness of light replaced by harsh fluorescent. Huught looked at me sadly and dipped his head in reverence of our last moment. Looking at his hand I saw the small orange flower shrink, wither, and fall to the ground, turning to ashes as it made contact. It was time to stand. My knees threatened to avoid their duty, but the lightness of the rest of me floated upward and succumbed. We looked at each other's eyes for the last moment allowed before taking our places in the line and descending from a heaven which the guards could not notice or steal away from us. And before the call for silence broke our private moment, we thanked each other.

The room went quiet and they formed us back into the line. My steps had a euphoric float to them, but I tried not to show it on the outside. The rec-room was no place for intimacy, but the situation had been unique, and free from touch. But it could never be let known to the guards; they would kill Huught without hesitation. Probably me as well. So I put my head forward and one slow foot in front of the other, and marched with the rest back down the long hall to the mess.

Food, if you can call it that, almost always came after our exercise and social time. I say almost because sometimes these meals were skipped, whether as a form of punishment or not, we didn't know. No explanations were ever given, nor was there a discernible pattern. Personally, I believed that it had something to do with disruptions outside rather than some internal situation with the inmates, but had no way to prove anything one way or another. Today, they marched us straight to the mess. We sat in our designated places. These only changed if someone was removed or killed. The room was blank as the rest, slate gray, tables bolted to the cement floor. Only a small slot in the wall that dispensed our trays of slop from an unseen hand or machine. But the air was tense and stale. Even though we were supposed to look down at our food while we ate, several times I saw other inmates stealing glances at me. It was forbidden, but they were chancing it, either in awe at the stunt I had pulled, or resentful of so brazen a scoff at the guards. I sensed it was the latter, it had been a dangerous move to have sex so openly outside of our cells, but could the guards have recognized it for what it was? Hell, I wasn't even sure that sex was the right word for what we had done. But intimacy, yeah, they probably could have spotted it, if they knew what they were looking for. But they had not, and no evidence was left behind except for my weakened legs and slightly less weight on my back. Perhaps those looks were ones of envy and I could only pity them. It's so hard to tell sometimes with alien faces and expressions. It's hard enough to tell with another human. So I stopped trying to guess, looked down, and ate.

The food was a thick dry paste, somehow moister on the outside than on the inside. It left everything to be desired. It was hard to identify which was worse, the taste or the texture. But you ate or you didn't, so we all choked it down. Hunger strikes would get you nowhere. We'd seen it before, a desperate inmate losing hope or in protest, and they'd just let him starve, no matter how long it took. There's nothing worse than watching a man wither like that, becoming a ghost right before you, he having no way to end it but still refusing. I suppose there is something valiant in this action, but oh god is it painful to watch, especially in enforced silence. So, I ate. We all did. None enjoying it, but because you go on living no matter what, if for no other reason than to deny them the pleasure of being there at the end of a short life. To make future shit for them to clean up. For many of us, life itself was the protest. They may have trapped us and taken everything, but some of us refused to give up that most important and elusive quality for a place like this – dignity.

Our captors were not overly specific in their tactics of dehumanization, and I suppose it would have been difficult to do so given the wide variety of species imprisoned, and even wider variety of living condition preferences. One man's shit is another man's breathable atmosphere, and all that. Stifling freedom of mobility and freedom of stimuli were their main fronts of attack, and these, without doubt, affected every species in negative ways. Apparently, every intelligent species evolved to run and move about, and invoke curiosity. It was difficult to tell if the prison was an ingenious reduction of punishment to an art, or if it was simply designed for efficiency. The architecture, the routines, all said next to nothing about our captors or their motives. During social time there was much conjecture, especially among the newer arrivals, but the theories were circular, often recycled, and gave no real insights into our position. I remember the days when I had desperately sought answers and did everything I could to find out, but it was better to just be alive. Life is hope enough without clinging to false hopes, or a lifer's confused, cobbled together, hairbrained schemes. Still, thoughts of escape ran through me constantly. I'm sure they ran through everybody, how could they not? Even if one did their best to accept circumstance it never got easier, and some days were worse than others. Today had been one of the better ones, no death, no fights. This was the most one could ask for in a place like this.

When the thoughts of escape couldn't be resisted anymore, they would always lead back to the anonymous captors. To know the prison one had to know them, and we didn't. How many times had I, had we, gone over it? The same information and the same conclusions, sometimes garnished with wild fantasy, or ludicrous embellishment solely for the purpose of not arriving at the same results yet again, but the conversations and speculations always ended the same way. All that we truly knew of those that imprisoned us was their prison and their guards, both of which yielded little information.

We knew they could build androids and prisons, that much was clear. The variable light cycles and the occasional shifts in gravity could be a clue to their origins, and we'd been round and round that one... But it was equally likely that those aspects of this place were merely part of the punishment. How much does a building say about its creator? Lots, but that is if they have built it for themselves. Our current home was clearly designed with a multitude of species in mind, from the oversized doors (for myself, at least), to the rumored wings for non-oxygen breathers. All with the complete lack of windows. Most beings craved the light and so this could be one more form of punishment, or we could simply be underground somewhere, or as I suspected, loose in space or on a ship or asteroid or something. The latter was the only way I could reconcile the variance in gravity. It didn't happen often but sometimes a shift would occur, and a lethargy would take over the inmates, as if we all strained under higher G forces. But they could also be altering our atmospheric mix, it was hard to say, especially since these moments did nothing for clarity of mind, leaving almost all of us disorientated. Hence the circular nature of our search for answers. It drove many to avoid the subject altogether. The speculation did little to comfort anyone, and more often than not, could drive a man to madness, only to be dragged away screaming, never to been seen again.

Our bunking cells were kept cold. One couldn't say if it was a form of climate control, or lack thereof. But for most of us they were kept too cold to be comfortable, making it difficult to sleep. Some species didn't mind at all, actually preferred it, but they were in the minority. The bunks were stiff, hard metal, no pillows of course, and while they did give us small squares of fabric to cover ourselves, they weren't by any stretch of the imagination blankets. And they did little to fight off the pervasive cold.

After mess, which was always an unpleasant affair - one had to learn to ignore the eating habits of others as well as gagging down the "food" - the guards would oversee our cleaning of the place, not just the trays and tables but also the entire kitchen. With so many of us this usually went quickly and it was a good thing it came after eating because the sight of the kitchen was enough to kill any appetite. I pitied the guys who worked in there full time and thanked luck that my work duties were elsewhere. Of course they rotated us, so I'd end up in the kitchen sooner or later. Hopefully later.

After the collective cleansing of the mess and kitchen they would march us down more long, blank halls. I had often, as had many of my fellow inmates, attempted to count every step and try to figure out the size of the prison. But many of the walls curve slightly, things would happen that made me lose count, or they'd make some unexpected change and switch the floor we were on, so none of us had ever been able to put together an accurate picture of the size or shape of the prison. It was one of the many things that dashed hopes of escape. How could we find a way out if we didn't even know anything about where or what was on the outside of those walls. All the conjecture in the universe wouldn't help prepare someone for a getaway, especially if it was hard vacuum on the other side, as I often imagined.

Through all of this marching, switching floors, single file pat downs, and short breaks for head counts – speaking was still forbidden. Many of us had developed small vocabularies of sign, but any notice from the guards brought broken fingers, so we reserved its use for the rec-room, or maybe in the mess if one was daring enough. All one heard was marching steps and cold air being circulated. It left one mad for want of stimuli and I would often pretend that the vents were a cool spring breeze and the footfalls were those of carnival going crowds hurriedly heading toward the rides. Those musings could never last and did nothing to comfort me. It felt like a cruel joke to even try. So, I would think about, and try to determine, what fantasies of home might be running through the minds of my fellow inmates as we marched. I could come up with many a bizarre scenario, but no matter how much I stretched my imagination I knew I had to be far from the truth – if only I could have asked – the variety of men here was too great to even scratch the surface of the truth of what their lives had been like in freedom. I imagined families, jobs, homes – but could never know what life would actually look like on so many worlds. The cosmos was obviously rich with variation and what a terrible vantage to be seeing it through a pinhole in a concrete box. It made me feel like a trapped animal, cut off from all beauty and only allowed to see the top layer of bestial suffering which we all shared in common.

The guards unceremoniously threw us into our new cells. More of a shove than being thrown, but either way we hit the back wall, not even seven feet from the door. The door shut automatically once we were inside.

A horrible thud, the sound of further confinement. The guards were always rough for this part of the day.

"You damned coward bastards!" I called after them when the door was shut. It was also the only time of the day when it was safe to shit talk the guards. They were either too lazy or too efficient to open the door back up to deliver a beating. Or they thought of it as a ruse to get them to open the door, but either way it was the only time one could express vocal opposition toward them.

My cellmate didn't look as though he approved of my tactic, and he certainly didn't join in as others might. Every night a different cell and a different cellmate. I couldn't see any other purpose for the constant reassignment. I tried to get as familiar with every cell as possible but as far as I could tell I had never been in the same one twice, and lights out was so soon after the clatter of doors closing that there was hardly enough time to explore the mundane features of our cell block rooms. Those with blindfolds probably had a better idea of the cells, but I had yet to bunk with one of them.

And tonight it was, "Looks like it's just you and me," I extended my hand to greet my cellmate and in return was met with something between a hand and a claw, with fingers that bent backwards through some strange configuration of the knuckles. It had taken a while to learn to overlook such superficial traits, a hand was a hand – still, we were more similar than some. It could still be difficult to overcome when there was no "hand" to shake. Either way, this human gesture of greeting was lost on most, it was more of an indication that the individual had interacted with a human before than anything else.

The rest of him had the same slick cold texture like that of his hand, similar to reptile scales but somehow softer to the touch. He was more or less humanoid, but also sported a short tail.

His expression was unreadable and didn't seem to change. "Humans. Always shouting at guards. Does something satisfying? Guards seldom notices. So somethings withouts points."

"Have to let off steam while you can. Not like there's many opportunities around here. Even a small sliver of defiance can help keep us alive."

"Steam saves lives. Places without sun shiver. Cells freezes. Colders is soon. Without suns."

The poor man was cold blooded. And as lights out approached the temperature in the cells would plummet. I got the feeling that the small slivers of blankets provided would not be enough, even if I sacrificed mine for his cause. I could see why he had found my small act of defiance to be pointless. He had bigger problems; I wondered how many nights he had endured coming close to freezing to death, if he had watched others of his kind perish in the lonely night of our cold cells. I reminded myself not to complain of the cold again, even if I was bunked with another human. How many things become trivial when faced with how they affect others. The prison was a different kind of hell for each species.

If he was worried about making it through the night it did not show on his face, but he kept moving as if to keep his blood circulating for as long as possible. Hell, it was probably too cold for him before the lights went out and the temperature dropped.

"Let's move, my friend. Before the lights are out." I suggested.

The look he returned said nothing to me, unreadable. And he said nothing. I led with jumping jacks, attempting to raise my body temperature. He followed suit, but the hinges of his limbs did not allow for the same motion and his movements were an odd parody of mine. But we moved together in a physical gesture of solidarity. I didn't know if it did anything to ease his oncoming suffering, but to not be alone in his ailment seemed to take his mind off of the coming discomfort. And the lights snapped off.

At lights out the cells became pitch black. No light whatsoever. At least for human eyes it was impossible to see, and one had to use their hands to find their way around the cell to the small bolted down cots.

"Human eyes seeing darkens."

He was actually concerned for me even though his issue was infinitely more urgent.

"It's the least of our troubles, friend."

I found my cot after groping around. He probably would have found it amusing if not for the cold. His eyes clearly didn't have as difficult a time as his body in adjusting. I gathered up the excuse for a blanket and patted the cot next to my body, signaling him to join me. The gesture seemed to go over his head.

"Join me. The cold is not an issue for my body. I can share my heat."

He emitted a small sound. I couldn't tell if it was relief or disgust. But he crawled onto the cot, barely big enough for one, and spooned his body up to mine. I threw the little square of blanket on top of us, and he did the same with his. I knew it must have helped, for he nestled up closer to me, making as much contact as possible. His cold flesh felt foreign, but its smoothness still had an erotic effect. I turned over and brought my arms around him, bringing him in as close as possible. A rumbling in his throat confirmed that my warmth brought with it some slight relief.

Eventually the rhythm of the sound became regular and as far as I could tell he had fallen asleep in my arms. His skin remained cold, and I shivered as I lay there unable to go to sleep myself. It would be a long night, but one he could live through. How he had made it through however many nights he had been here I could not say, but it felt as though our solution could only work with certain arrangements. It felt good for my body to have a use in this strange place of discomfort and suffering. And maybe that's why they rotate us, to prevent us from finding ways to help each other through the torment. They had taken everything from me, from us, and still my body had worth, if only to help another man keep warm in the insufferable cold of night. Something primal that could not be taken from us, and as mammalian as the gesture was, he understood immediately.

As he slept I watched over him, unable to see anything and uncertain if it was preferable not to see. Unlikely as our closeness was, it was certainly a victory over our captors, another small thing they could not steal away from us. He slept like a child and remained a man despite their icy lack of caring for what a man went through merely to survive another night. They could try to dehumanize us, but in that moment, there was nothing more human than what we were doing, helping to keep each other warm in genuine caring embrace.

In the morning his face was still unreadable and although I hadn't slept, I felt better than I did the day before. Part of me was grateful for the night's darkness as I looked at him, but then felt horrible for having such a thought. Regardless of his exterior, or how different it was from my own, he was a person. One who could see in the dark. And despite how grotesque I might look to him, and I surely did, he had never once judged me. Which is as it should be. I was ashamed even though I had helped him, as we now stood face to face. Of course, I had not acted upon such petty impulse, but to have thought it at all was embarrassing.

I had lived long enough to know what makes a man a man.

That thinking, which had crept into me, was exactly what our captors would have happen and it was possibly one of their reasons for never giving us more than one night with a bunkmate. To keep us alone and fearful of one another, and damn them for infecting me with even the briefest moment of bigotry. No matter how different the man I had spent the night with might look, he was still a man.

Once again, I stuck my hand out, this time as a farewell. He shook his head, and I could not understand why until I saw that his tail was extending toward me. Reaching to shake this extremity he shook his head again, leaving me confused. Until the prehensile tail found its way to my pants and unclasped them. This gesture was not lost on me, and I rose as he found his way and curled around me. The tail was cold and slick, but in such a way that my arousal grew along with my member. He made quick work of it, and it was hard to believe that he might not have done this before. His movements were deft and brought me to climax within minutes, spraying my finish onto the floor between us. It brought with it a relief that sleep could not, and I regretted that this would be our last moment, that I had no time to repay the kindness.

As we looked at each other to say our goodbyes I could let all of that conditioning go and see him for the beautiful man that he was, scales and all, his strange yellow eyes held tenderness no matter how reptilian and foreign to me. Whoever had put us in this hell would not win today, for though the ugliness that they bestowed upon us could not cover up something greater, all of their irregular darkness could not blind us to the hearts of other men. And we were unified in a way they could never be: each of us longed for our freedom, and that is a thirst which drives something in a man which should not be trifled with. No matter what they did they could not make this man ugly, and no one could take away our night together. And as the sirens wailed and called us off to the mess, we were shoved into different lines and lost sight of each other. Only then did I realize that we had not exchanged names, which saddened me. But we had exchanged something much bigger, something which I would not soon forget.

My line trailed off down one of the endless hallways and the lights seemed brighter than usual, enough so that I wanted to shield my eyes but did not for the guards tolerated no deviations in the form of the line. I told myself it was the lack of sleep, and winced to try and let less of the ugly light in. At one point closing my tired eyes for a moment and nearly bumping into the guy in front of me; fortunately, I opened them in time not to make the blunder. It could have been a fatal mistake and I breathed a deep breath of the foul air to try and wake me. As gentle as the night had been, today would be harsh, and any comforts the night had brought were gone now. Back to their routines; any deviations would bring about one of their calculated punishments. A night in the hole was not worth it. And I didn't even want to think about what else they could do to poison the feelings of comradery that were warming me this morning. So, I was a good prisoner and I marched, hoping that whatever slop was in the mess this morning would snap me into alertness, that no matter how nasty, the calories would bring some comfort to my aching body, and that the glow I felt in that moment would go unnoticed by the guards. The best I could hope for was a morning of anonymity. Like everyone else I kept my head down, looking at my feet, and remembering the times when I could run freely if that was what my feet and heart desired. But today there would be no running, no freedom of the heart. But if I was lucky, the coming night might offer the latter in some way, no matter how alien.

The line was solemn as it moved down the hall. The

guards seemed tense; it had the inmates even more tense. It was palpable and it made the atmosphere in the halls thicker than usual. No one made a sound, in even greater fear of the guards than usual. Did they know something? Had something happened on another block? They wouldn't be telling us. They never told us anything except where to go and when. And one didn't dare to ask. The one time a man did, I saw them smash his face in before taking him away, never to be seen again. So no one asked.

I couldn't imagine what could be different about today. This place changed so little, barely any deviation from the routines. Any abrupt changes here, no matter how subtle, got a man thinking, and usually for the worse. My mind was reeling already, fearing that a punishment awaited me for the affection I had shown last night. The fact that I hadn't slept wasn't helping. The tension had me paranoid and I could tell by those in line around me that I wasn't the only one. But the guards said and did nothing but usher us down the hall to the mess, following the usual routine, the only change being so subtle that an outsider, or a new arrival, might not have noticed it at all.

My mind went to opportunities of escape. Perhaps there had been one on another block. Or an invasion... A visiting supervisor... A cargo ship full of new prisoners... My mind swirled with all of the possibilities for what could have caused the change, but at best it was pointless guessing. And for all of the excitement welling up in me I saw no valid opportunities for escape. Besides, where would I possibly go? Back to the bunks... The rec? There wasn't anywhere to go, at least not that I had ever seen. But the relentlessness was real and I could feel it spilling through the crowd, which in turn put the guards on another level of alert. It was a dangerous feedback loop, one that would probably get someone killed. It had been over a week since the last death, a good long run, so I suppose we were overdue. But it never did a man any good. You'd get to thinking about your own death, and in this place that was a dark poison to be avoided. It was too easy to get yourself killed to be dancing around with those kinds of thoughts. And suicide by guard was all too common. At least amongst those who had been here long enough to know how little the prison changed over time. I was now one of those guys. But I did my best to keep that pessimism at bay. I told myself to roll with it, no matter how terrible things became. I'd outlived many and that had to say something about my resilience. Didn't it? No answer would come, not in the silence of the line. And the guards sure weren't going to be giving out pats on the back any time soon.

Tense as it was, we made our way down the hall to the mess without incident. It was a miracle that no violence had erupted with that kind of energy pulsing through the air. The tension with the guards had not gone anywhere, but we tried to ignore it as we got our trays out of the slots and set about filling up with to-day's tasteless and mushy calories.

The contents of the tray looked awful. But no better or worse than any other meal I'd had here. It was nourishment of some sort and that was all that mattered. I wondered if it was worse for some of the other species. I could imagine that for some it didn't even provide the base essentials. No matter what, I had to eat. It had been a while since they had me on wash duty, and I figured they'd have me back on it any day. But I wouldn't be asking and there'd be no upcoming schedule posted; I just had to be ready. So I made my way to the assigned seat to get mealtime over with.

The tension was still there, only ever so slightly diffused from the food. Looking around, everything was as usual. All of us in our places, eating in silence, and the guards ringing the room. When did those guys eat? Did they have to? I put my eyes back on my plate. No use getting caught staring at them and losing an eye or something worse. They didn't notice me looking at them or my quick look away. It felt like something was up. Were they distracted? What good would it do me even if they were? My heart leapt with excitement that something could happen, some break in routine, but it could only end in violence if something occurred. And with the extra tension this morning it would be bad. Or maybe I only felt that way from lack of sleep. It wouldn't be the first time my senses perked up only to report nothing. I tried to stop worrying about it and eat.

My tray lifted ever so slightly. I really hadn't slept enough. It hovered just above the table, not enough to pass a finger under it, but it was definitely not making contact with the table. I thought my mind was gone until I heard collective gasping as my fellow inmates found themselves in the same position. The guards began to stir at the noise. They all took a step closer, away from the wall, ringing us in. They had felt it too and held their positions, ready should something start. The gravity was wrong again. But this time it wasn't stronger G forces... we were lighter. The realization rippled through the room. We weren't in freefall but something strange was happening. Other times, when the gravity had increased without warning, I had figured it was due to acceleration, adding to my supposition that we were on some kind of prison ship enroute somewhere. But this was no acceleration. And it could only be caused by something in space... or not. As much as I wanted to contemplate the answer it would serve me better to try and stay in my seat and keep an eye on those around me and the guards. It was moments like these that people did something crazy.

Sharp angle turns? Sudden deceleration? I wanted to know but now my stomach was in my throat and the challenge of keeping the food down ramped up to a whole new level. And then it was over. The guards stepped back to their places on the wall and nothing was said, no explanation offered, or even an acknowledgement of our change in environment. But the uneasiness remained, worse now and thickening the air with the smell of fear. Something had happened. I could see on the faces of the other inmates that some of us were trying to piece together this new clue with speculations about our location, and potential for escape. Wheels turned in all of those heads but I doubted any of us were getting much closer to the truth.

We finished eating and fortunately the small lapse in gravity wasn't enough to make a mess of the place. And even though there was no more to clean up than usual they marched us right out of there before we had done any cleaning. I'd never seen that happen before; nervous glances were exchanged all around. Was there something they didn't want us to see? Was it being left up to the kitchen crew? Something to do with the gravity shift? We weren't marching toward the rec or elsewhere; they were taking us back to our cells. I had figured they'd be working me today since never more than two or three days passed without labor. Apparently that was canceled or postponed. It wasn't like them to deviate from routine, but it also wasn't like they posted schedules or let us know what was going to happen. You just got used to this place and began to feel its rhythms, or at least I had after so long.

Back to the cells it was, and as ever we were paired up with different bunkmates. Mine was a species I had never seen before. And he looked at me with equal curiosity and surprise. Apparently he was also a stranger to humans. He was tall, a good foot higher than me, so that I had to look up to see his face. His exterior appeared to be an exoskeleton, something I had not seen up until now; I could barely guess at his physiology or the paths evolution would have to take to make such a body type. He gestured in our simple prison sign to sit on the bunk, but we clearly weren't going to be able to have any in-depth discussion about what had happened in the mess. No doubt it was on both of our minds though. He signed the word for friend and I did the same. At least we had nothing to worry about from each other. We sat in silence, which was fine with me as I was trying to figure out what could have caused such an alteration in gravity, such a subtle change but with huge implications. I don't think it could have happened if we were planet bound. Unless maybe we were under-water... It was maddening to know so little about this damned place. And every little bit of info just raised more questions. And we all had the same story; none of us could remember being put in here. Not me, not my new crabbish friend, no one. You just woke up in one of these cells one day and figured out the routines or you were dragged away screaming. My friend here seemed to know the drill, so it was sort of strange that I had never seen his kind, but I had long suspected that the prison was much bigger than any of us realized. And now this sudden departure from routine...

My bunkmate and I were doing our best to have a conversation about the change but were ill-equipped in our vocabulary to be very specific. As foreign as his features were, I could read frustration there, and I think he could recognize the same in mine for he threw out a sign of sympathy. I returned the gesture. And then the lights snapped off.

It was the shortest interval of lights on that I had experienced since my arrival. And I had been here for a considerable amount of time. How long, I didn't know. But it was long. Did they expect us to go back to sleep? I was tired from the previous "night," so in a way it was welcome. But something serious must have happened to alter the schedule this drastically. No explanation was going to come but they had rounded us up for a reason and I suspected that being thrown back into our cells wasn't the end of it. The blankets must have been taken away to the wash while we were on our way to the mess because there were none in the cell. Just cots. And it was cold already. I groped my way through the darkness to the cot and my eyes drooped as soon as I laid my body down. I said good night to my cellmate even though it was probably a meaningless sound to him. I was quickly out.

When I awoke the lights were still out. I couldn't know how long I had slept but I felt well refreshed, so it must have been a while. The room was also still cold; I knew I had to have slept deeply not to have been awakened by it. It was silent and disorientating, so I called out, "Hello? Am I alone?"

My voice was met with a chittering sound which I took to mean, "I'm here."

The darkness made the room feel huge and my cellmate distant, even though his voice was close. I stood to approach him, needing answers but unable to understand his words, hoping we could sign in the dark, not knowing if he could see me or not. Within steps I was at his side and reaching out felt his shoulder. It was hard as a shell and cold to the touch, but not altogether unpleasant, like touching a river polished stone. Its smoothness almost made it feel soft. He did not flinch at my touch, making me think he might be able to see me.

At my touch he stood up as well. I could feel him near to me and was uncertain what to do next. He took care of that and wrapped his arms around me. They were cold but something opened in his stomach and chest revealing a softer, warmer interior. It was an odd but sensuous contrast to the shell. I pulled off my shirt. Our flesh made contact as it fell away. The warmth of my front against the cold of my backside was somehow pleasing and he gathered me further in. He held me like that for a moment before we backed away without a word and dropped what was left of our uniforms.

Beneath his pants was nothing like the shell, a soft tender underside came against me and it was sweet relief from the cold that permeated the room. This was soon forgotten as his soft interior enveloped me. His flesh consumed my lower half. We rippled together in an unfamiliar but pleasing sensation.

And the gravity went away again, this time completely. Our feet lifted from the floor and together we floated toward the ceiling. In the dark it was as if we had drifted off into the void and there was nothing left but our embrace. It was serene. The most private moment I had experienced since being dumped in this hell. But none of that seemed to matter now. There was a dampness where our flesh met, welcoming and drawing me further in with a pleasant subtle scent which I could not place. So, without movement, suspended in midair, we exchanged pleasure so intimately in a way I had never imagined. The intensity grew in ways I did not know how to reciprocate. But his pleasure also felt complete. His soft chittering expressed the equivalent of cooing, so I knew the overwhelming sensation was taking us both. His arms were now open, and though I could not see the gesture I could feel it as some sort of climax, his release. And mine came too. I came.

In the freefall of zero G my body slowly flew away from his with each spasm of pleasure. Equal and opposing force. Ever so slowly my body jetted away from his as we undocked and my body made its way through the air, hitting the wall on the other side of the room, unceremoniously knocking me loose from the experience. At that moment the lights snapped on and the gravity returned, dropping our naked bodies to the floor in an unexpected jolt. For the first time we got a really good look at each other, and what we saw was strange, but comforting and real.

Hitting the floor was the least alarming aspect of what was going on. There was now no doubt in my mind, we had to be in space. And something drastic enough was going on to have the routines altered more than usual. It had to be more than a play to keep us off kilter. They had put us back in our cells to avoid the chaos that would have broken out if the gravity had fully cut when we were all out. What happened in the mess had only been a stutter, a precursor to whatever had caused what had just happened. And there we were floating around the room like a couple of boys at space camp, getting all flirty at our first float. But despite all that, for the first time there was some concrete proof about what was really going on. Our prison had become a little less mysterious, but no less terrifying. We were in space.

And knowing that we were in space begged the question, were we going somewhere? And if so, why? The horrible thought dawned on me: if this was a ship and we were moving, how far had we traveled since my arrival? There was no way to tell time and I'd long since lost count of the days but it had to be a year, almost a year, more? I couldn't be sure. But it was long enough to have traveled a great distance. And I had already been far from home. It might be a ship, but how fast was it moving? Their control of gravity was not centrifugal, so they had to be advanced beyond belief. Damn if knowing we were in space did anything but create more questions. And as I looked into my friend's face, I could tell that the same thoughts were running through his mind, and no matter how different our bodies and faces were, it was obvious that he liked the conclusion about as much as I did.

Before we could attempt to express our feelings to each other the lights went back out. And then back on.

And then several more times. There was no timing to the flicker which made me think 'malfunction'. Or was it to further disorient us? Through routine and subtle variation. The tactic was starting to make sense, but nothing about the last few minutes came across as deliberate. This felt wrong.

A guard burst into our cell, and ignoring my cellmate prodded me with his stick in the gesture that meant only one thing. Work duty. He completely ignored my friend as he ushered me out of the room, alone, into the hall. And I dared not look back and catch a last glimpse of my friend before we were separated forever.

The guard was rough, as usual, but not overly so. It sent a message: this wasn't punishment, it was a scheduled shift. Or at least it was designed to look so. Typically they would march us out together and separate us down various halls to our respective work places for the day. Something was different about this, because the guard had left my bunkmate in the cell and the door had shut behind us. Why? What were their plans for him? The answer to that question meant less and less as I was marched down the hall and through a door I had never seen, into a part of the prison that was altogether foreign to me. It filled me with terror as this was the biggest change in routine that I had yet to experience during captivity. The demeanor of the guard had not changed. But something had. I started to question whether I was on my way to work duty, or an execution. We were alone in this new hall, which was a first in and of itself, and it couldn't mean anything good.

I was shocked when we entered a small room with only one door, and then it started moving. An elevator. The first I had ever seen here. My dread rose up to my throat as we descended. I didn't know of, and had never heard anyone speak of, lower floors to the prison, or any other floor at all. The guard's face remained placid and unreadable as ever. He never turned away from me and stood like a vigilant statue in his watch.

Either we were moving really slowly or descending really far. There was no display in the elevator car to indicate which. As much as I tried to get my bearings and pinpoint my location it was useless. This damn building had so little visual diversity it practically looked the same everywhere. Aside from the size of the car it could have been anywhere in the prison. Being alone with a guard troubled me deeply. Even when they had pulled me aside for a disciplinary beating for speaking in the mess there had been two of them, and they took care of it right there in the hall with no reason to parade me around.

Mentally I tried to prepare to defend myself. I had nothing but my hands, but perhaps I could free the guard of his prod. While that might stop him momentarily, I doubted I would make it very far once more guards were alerted. So I waited. And I wondered if we had gone really far or if time had slowed down in my state of fear. For all I knew the whole thing could be an act and we were in a broom closet with someone shaking the wall. I wouldn't put it past them in this scant culture of paranoia and stripping one of their self. But the door opened. It was an elevator. My fears shifted focus. We stepped out into another hall and this one was nothing like the others. The light was different. The tone of the endless gray was different. It was a shock to my eyes. There had been too little variation for too long and I could barely register what I was seeing.

Everything in me seized up. My feet were like weights until the guard rammed his stick into my back and spurred me from my inaction. We proceeded down this foreign hall, my heartbeat rapidly expecting my life was to end in moments. And then the hall opened up into a large room. The biggest I had yet to see anywhere during my confinement. With another startling difference, it was populated with large cylinders and tubing that ran in every which way. It could have been an engine room or a septic processing plant, I had no idea. It was also darker than the rooms above. The lighting was diffuse and its source impossible to ascertain. Nothing about the place was welcoming.

He scuttled me into a corner. This was it. My muscles tensed. My mouth went dry. I prepared for the blow. But it didn't come. He pointed with his prod to a cabinet built into the wall and gestured for me to open it. His silence was unnerving, as was his ever-unchanging expression. There was nothing to do but obey, so I opened the door to find it was a supply closet. It was filled with several tools, none of which I had seen before. The panic of my death subsided and was replaced by a fear and uncertainty of what was expected of me now. I looked back at the guard, but his face said nothing. He indicated one of the tools, so I dutifully reached for it. A broom-like handle that terminated in a broad, flat scraping implement. For the first time since my arrival I held a weapon in my hands; images flashed in my mind of beheading the guard where he stood. My mind was racing without clarity. Normally, in a situation of violence I would let my mind clear and my muscles relax, but my being would not allow for any of that. I was stiff as a board and taut as a hanging rope with its latest victim dangling.

In that moment I knew what a futile and suicidal move any attack would be. His face remained unchanged as he made a motion with his prod, a vague gesture that suggested the use of the tool. So, I mirrored him and scraped at the calcified buildup that covered much of the floor. He gave an almost imperceptible nod and also pointed at the cylinders. So, this was to be my task. I continued scraping. Seemingly satisfied he turned and walked back toward the elevator, a door that had gone unnoticed before it shut behind him sealing off the room. I was alone. For the first time in this godforsaken place, I was alone.

The lights never dimmed or turned off, nor did anyone come or go. If this was a work duty, or a punishment, I still couldn't say. I'd been in the hole before, but that was a dark, small room. This place had some sort of function, though it was difficult to say what that might be. I resolved to use my time here to find out. The prison had revealed at least one of its secrets; perhaps more were to be found. The scraping implement made a horrible high-pitched whine every time it made contact with the floor as I attempted to remove the buildup. It wasn't much of an incentive to get the job done. But there was no telling when they would return, and when they did, if the place wasn't tidied to their satisfaction who knew what the response might be. I wasn't going to tempt fate and find out. But neither did they give me any reason to do a good job. Trying to pass with the minimum effort made the most sense. And it would give me time to look for answers. Typically, outside of the cells there were no unsupervised movements, and from what I could tell the place also lacked cameras. So, I would scrape for a while and then look around, alternating every few minutes. When I looked around, I would drag the tool behind me in hopes that it sounded like the work continued. There was no way to know if they were listening either.

Much of the large room was the same. Cylinders lined the walls and also formed rows throughout the place. The ceilings were the highest I had seen anywhere in the prison. And it had a strange odor. It wasn't the tarnish that I had been tasked with cleaning but something metallic mixed with disuse. And water, like being near a river that's just out of sight. The arrangement did little to hint at its use, and as far as I could tell the automatic door was the only entry or exit point.

That and the little hole in the floor, barely big enough for a hand, where I had been scraping the muck into. There was no getting through there, and although I had not been instructed to use it, it was the only logical place to dispose of the buildup. There was a purpose to this place, and presumably my task. I had to find out. I inventoried what I knew, which was little. But the incident with the gravity suggested much. It hinted at what this place might be.

As much as I wanted answers, I was getting tired and hungry. They had ended our last meal before we could eat, and with the endless dim light cycle here I did not know how much time had passed. My stomach said that I had missed two or three meals. But I didn't dare sit down to rest, for if the guard returned and I wasn't working, there would be punishment. Still, I was slowing down. As much as I sought answers my clarity was leaving me in my fatigue.

Thinking that a change of position might help, my back was killing me from leaning over to scrape the floor, I moved to the cylinders lining the wall in hopes that working a different set of muscles might wake me up a bit. When the scraper met the metal, it became obvious that the cylinders were tanks. Beating my palm against the side it was apparent that it was filled with liquid. Walking down the rows I tested them all and each rang with a similar dull thud. They were all full. A slight background hum suggested that the liquid was circulating. And then it clicked. If this was the plumbing system for the prison then I would have expected some of the tanks to only be partially filled as the water would be in use. But all of them making the same sound implied a different use. If the prison was truly a ship then perhaps I was near the outer hull and the liquid was being circulated though the exterior walls of the ship in order to block radiation. It made more sense than anything else I could glean. Or my exhausted mind was merely desperate for answers. I went back to scraping, unsure of how much time had passed in my contemplation, and still fearing the return of the guard. What little evidence I had all pointed toward the prison being a craft, but what good did the information do to help me or my fellow inmates? It certainly wasn't a comforting thought as far as potential escape was concerned. And unless I could shrink to get through the drainpipe there was no getting out of this room until they came to shuffle me off to whatever they had in mind for me after this task.

So I kept scraping the best I could, knowing that there was no reward for good behavior but that things could certainly get worse. I tried to enjoy the solitude, for outside of the hole there was no alone time, but somehow I had grown accustomed to the men here that I now consider brothers, friends, and some of them lovers.

Hunger and fatigue were descending upon me with increasing vigor. Neither option had a viable solution. If they were going to bring food it would have happened by now. If I slept and the guard returned it would not end well. But I couldn't take it any longer. I needed some relief from standing, no matter how brief. How many hours, days, had I been without food or sleep? My stomach had one answer, my mind another. And they refused to agree in my exhaustion. I fought and fought but if I did succumb then I would collapse.

Using the scraping tool as a crutch I made my way to the corner, one that I had already cleaned, and let myself down to sit. At least with two walls at my back there was a slim chance of being alerted to the approach of a guard. They couldn't come at me from behind.

My eyes were drooping and heavy and only the horrible lighting prevented them from shutting all the way. Merely being off my feet put me in a state of blissful gratitude, but one which I knew to be false and could not last. Sleep kept threatening to take me. I wanted it so bad but through my fatigue I could see clearly that it would be a sleep from which I would not awake. I imagined them coming in, seeing me there, attempting to rouse me with their prods, and if that failed, doing me in with a clean blow to the head. It would all be over before I knew it had begun, and while there was a certain appeal to that, I wasn't ready to die yet. Not like that, not here. But in the desperation of sleeplessness, sleep's allure was powerful and treacherous, calling me to the ground. I dared not lay down. There would be no fighting it if I did. The inner cry for relief was so strong I had to do something.

And as the body's needs went unmet, as is often the case, another bodily need presented itself. I had experienced it once in the heat of battle. Once when nearly falling asleep at the wheel, so many years ago back on Earth. And now it came on stronger than hunger or sleep. Sex replaced all needs with something even more voracious and immediate. There was nothing sexy about my situation or surroundings but still I felt my stirring turn to rising. It was on me, demanding, stern and insistent. Of all the times to be possessed with such overwhelming floods of lust I was alone. Usually I could ask a friend for help but being on my own left no choice.

I reached a dirty hand down and freed myself from my pants. My heart sped up elevating me slightly from my stupor. It was no substitute for another, but it took me anyway. Earth was a distant abstraction as were memories of human lovers and as my brained flipped through these blank pages it quickly moved on to my time in this prison. The focus of faces of my lovers there, the nights which were the only comfort, the new ways of being I had been shown, the strange but wonderful touches, and the freedom we found in each other. Our captors could take everything but could never steal away the freedom of the mind, even when isolated in this awful room. A room which faded into previous experiences that rolled past my mind's eye in a rapid flipbook show of memory snippets. A hand, a face, limbs, touch, climax, entering, being entered, the various backs mounted, grunts and moans. The freedom of sex in a flood of feeling.

My hand worked with these pictures, the smells and sensations, and lost in these, worked with my body. I swelled. My hand was another, so many others, as the files of experience were pulled one after another and contrasted in quick erotic succession. The moving images matched the movement of my hand, rhythm overtaking me and spilling across the void I had traversed to end up here, a place which no longer existed. Hot breath in cold rooms. Silent faces in the halls not allowed to utter a word and needing to share in the freedoms of the night. And for the first time not hidden in the darkness of a cell I came and saw myself come. Solitary creation with no purpose other than lonely pleasure. Hunger and exhaustion fled in that moment as my muscles constricted and then finally relaxed, letting go of the strain of days of labor and uncertainty, replaced with the singular knowing of climax.

With great luck no guard had come to interrupt my private moment. My exhaustion was still present and nagging, but it was no longer pervasive and demanding. I resumed scraping in the nick of time. About ten minutes after starting up again, this time on the tanks, the automatic door opened to reveal the guard, prod already in hand. He strode into the room but did not directly approach me. I stood at attention, a cue that he had been seen and induced submission. Never turning his back toward me he circled the room inspecting the floor and tanks, checking my work. He moved slowly and deliberately as if the task had held great significance, and perhaps it did, though I could see no meaning or purpose in it. The room still looked filthy and disused, however, much less so now. Leaving no corner unchecked he made his rounds until, seemingly satisfied, he approached me face to face and pointed with his prod back toward the door. I had feared that he would hit me, for I still didn't know if my time in the tank room had been punishment for some unmentioned crime or merely an obscure work duty which I had not encountered before. His gesture suggesting it was over, at least for now, was ever welcome, and whatever came next, be it food or sleep, made me giddy with relief. It was hard to say which I wanted or needed more, but the thought of either could only have been outdone by the possibility of release.

Wearily, and with weakened legs, I obeyed his silent order and moved for the door. The room felt larger than when the door had been locked. And entering the hallway, even more so. It's easy to take space for granted until it's taken away from you. Now, it was back to the narrow halls and the small cells. There had been elbow room with no way to enjoy the sense of unconfined movement, or rather in my fear I had neglected to take advantage of it. Now my mind reeled with cartwheels, jumping jacks, twirling, and all manner of dance moves. How much we take simple pleasures of freedom for granted until they are taken away. I had let loneliness and fear of the guards take away a chance at leaping, running around the room. But then again, this was the point of the place. It had to be, because that's what it did to the psyche of every man imprisoned.

If the hallway had felt confining, the elevator was a ride of claustrophobia. Its walls seemed to bare down and get closer the farther the car ascended. The ride felt infinitely longer than it had during the descent, and I couldn't tell if we were headed to higher floors or if my delirium was getting the better of me. But I dared not collapse for fear of the rod. As usual my guard made not a sound and his looming figure brought no comfort even though it was a break in a solitude which had begun to consume me in awful ways. His presence suggested an impending violence, one for which I was defenseless, and it filled me with a longing to be among the other inmates. I could only pray that was where the car was taking us and not further into some hell of punishments that I had yet to imagine. As much as the desperation to ask consumed me the longer we stood there, voicing anything now could prove fatal and there was nothing to do but accept in silence whatever fate awaited me. When the door finally opened to a familiar, generic hallway it brought the sick relief of submission paying off.

There was no telling which floor we had arrived at, for the hall looked the same as all of the others. I could not tell if my perception of time had been skewed or if I was higher up than I had ever been. The hall was silent except for our footsteps echoing down the empty. I proceeded down the hall hoping to avoid the jab to the back that the guards loved so. Eventually I saw a door open to the rec-room, inmates ever circling inside. After all that time alone down below, it was a sweet relief to see people. One begins to think that they are truly alone, abandoned, or worse.

I didn't know if I could remain standing, let alone walking for exercise hour, but I doubted the guards would be giving me a choice. If it was exercise time, then hopefully food would soon follow. Hard to believe but my mouth actually salivated thinking of that sloppish excuse of a meal they call food. Hunger will change any perspective. I just had to make sure I didn't fall, and then the torment would go away. Ragged, moving like a zombie, the guard finally pushed me into the circle and the door closed.

Along with the others I circled and kept my head

down. My eyes were burning but I could see that there was another human in the room. I couldn't remember the last time I had seen one, let alone had an unbroken conversation completely in an Earth language. Hopefully the fellow spoke English. I had so many questions about what was going on, but didn't know after all this time whether my voice still worked. When was the last time I had spoken aloud?

But for now I circled, desperate for the break and the following mess time. When the call finally came to sit, I thought I might collapse. But the prisoner next to me, having seen this, came to my aid and helped me ease down. Getting off my feet was a brief flood of paradise, brief. The other human was across the room, so we couldn't speak, but made eye contact and nodded. The look on his face was the closest I had come to home since I couldn't say when. I was too exhausted to speak and the men around me paid no mind but quietly spoke to each other. Most of their words I couldn't make out or was just too tired to try. All the voices in the room were overwhelming after having nothing to listen to except the ringing in my ears and footsteps. It jumbled into a din, unpleasant, but at the very least helpful in keeping awake, for now I was battling and losing against sleep taking me right there. Something which the guards would absolutely not tolerate. And if something upset them, I might be denied my meal, a prospect I was unwilling to chance.

After an agony of time, they finally called us to stand. Those next to me had to help me up and they did so in silence, not questioning my condition. The other human made an attempt to get closer to me in line but failed to get less than a few places behind.

As we began marching my legs, my entire body, screamed inside for nourishment, but my mind was too cloudy to tell if we were headed for the mess or elsewhere. Everything looked the same in the ugly light of desperation. If only I could lean on the man in front of me, but that would have brought a swift beating to the both of us. One foot in front of the other was the best I could do. My body wanted nothing but to collapse in that moment. My legs screamed in revolt. My mind wanted to panic. My paranoia went to execution. And somehow all of that adrenaline kept me upright just long enough to make it through the hall to the mess. I sat in utter exhaustion, hardly believing that I had made it without incident.

Nothing seemed to have changed during my absence. The slop looked foul but it was the best meal I could ever remember having eaten. As much as I was tempted to, and it was difficult to stop myself, I forced myself to take it slowly and resisted the urge to cram it all in my mouth and swallow it whole. Who knew when they would feed me again, and I couldn't risk flashing up the meal by overworking my unused stomach. So, one spoonful at a time the food slowly entered me. And with every bite I slowly returned to being a man and the agony of the body started to release. As my awareness increased so did the lack of sleep present itself. It nagged persistently, annoyed at coming second to food. My body demanded its needs without care for prison routines and my mind fought against it with the knowledge of what could come next and how much worse punishments could be. The mix of desperation eventually slowed as the food reached my stomach and fortunately stayed down. How long had it been since my last meal which had been interrupted after only several bites? This time there was no disturbance in the gravity and all the men ate in silence as if nothing had ever happened.

As my clarity slowly improved, I scanned the faces of the inmates and the guards. The guards, of course, remained as blank as ever, expressionless and practically unreadable. The men were the usual blend of menagerie-like diversity, of all variety of species and from all parts of the galaxy and otherwise. Some species I recognized but as usual there were a few I couldn't identify, a daily reminder that the cosmos is grander than one could possibly imagine.

Most ate without looking up, but for me their faces were a forgotten comfort returning. Whether I knew them or not it was good to be amongst men again, for the scale of the universe also makes one lonely, almost more so than a small confining room.

I wondered if our captors also thought of us as men. Or were we merely animals to them, in a zoo for their entertainment. Our treatment suggested the latter, but to what ends? Could they reach such a level of advancement and still retain the old barbarities which so many cultures practiced? As a child I had seen pictures of the old zoos of Earth, complete with species so similar to our own, looking dejected and fully aware of their circumstance, aware of their enslavement. Here, with such a variety of beings, many of the faces were not as readable as those that had haunted me as a child. But it only took one look to know that this place brought suffering. That no species thrived in confinement. My cloudy mind raced at the cruelty. If I could have, I would have embraced every single prisoner and whispered an apology for something which I was not guilty of. It was good to know that they had been unsuccessful in killing my compassion, but still, there was no way to exercise it. And as I scanned all those faces, I met eyes with the only other human in the room. He returned a look of deep understanding. One that brought tears to my eyes.

That kind of thinking could make a man drop his guard at the wrong time and we weren't yet safely back in our cells. My mind was slipping from lack of sleep; I almost said so to the guy next to me, only stopping myself at the last moment. They would send me back down to that hole, or worse, for a talking violation. It felt like I was losing control of my faculties. The food had certainly taken the edge off of the desperation but now the fatigue was in charge. And it was demanding. The delirium began to tell me little stories filled with bad ideas about escape and attempting to take down the guards. Surely, they were outnumbered in the mess and, if we rose up with conviction, we could easily overtake the room. Then what? My mind refused to look that far into the possibility. My body revolted at the thought of violence, it was too exhausted even for pleasure. So I bit my tongue to prevent myself from voicing anything. So close to bunk time it was insanity to risk punishment. Sleep was a more appealing freedom in the moment.

Finally the call came and we rose to be marched off down the hallway. For a second my body refused to stand and only through internal mental battle was I able to overcome the revolt and follow the orders. Once standing I moved like a zombie, unaware of those around me, praying for a cot, and to not make any mistakes on the way to the cells. It passed in an abstract blur and I was in a cell; my cellmate spoke to me in un-accented English, full sentences and all. A bigger barrage of words than I had heard in so long. And I doubted them. I doubted my own ears. Something that familiar had lost its familiarity. All things were foreign. All men were strangers. All guards were enemies. How could something so home-like not be some cruel trick to deceive me into...into what? I could not register the voice as a truth and stumbled toward the cot, losing my footing on the way and falling to the floor. But I never hit.

His arms were around me, gingerly setting me down on the cot and tucking me in with both the cell's blankets. He hummed softly as he did this, and I wondered if this was the sound I had mistaken for English. But his face was human and so were his hands and his smell and his skin. It seemed like a lifetime since I had been bunked with another human, too long for me to remember having any verbal conversation at length, anyway. And as my heavy eyes began to refuse me their use, I feared that he was not real at all, and I was back in the room with the tanks. But he stroked my hair and continued to hum, soothing my delirious worry back into something manageable, back into the simple need for sleep instead of the nightmare scenarios that it was reaching for. I struggled one last time to get up and he gently held me down shushing me quietly.

"But...who are you? Why are you holding me down? Is this..."

His soft hands gave no threat but held firm. He leaned to whisper in my ear, and I felt his hot breath.

"It's time to sleep, my friend. Don't let them take this from you. It's the only place that it's safe to."

And I think he kept speaking in that beautiful tongue that I had almost forgotten, but I trailed off into a sleep that didn't care.

My eyes opened but the room was still black. I had not slept through the whole night but nevertheless was refreshed and the delirium had subsided. The sound of breathing was soft in the room but didn't suggest that my cellmate was asleep.

"Are you still there?"

"Yes. I've been watching over you. You were so exhausted that you thrashed around for a while but finally settled down. You were whispering in your sleep, but I couldn't make out what you were saying. Something about a ship. Are you sure you've slept enough? I think there's a few more hours till lights on."

His voice was gentle and kind, honey in a world of bitterness. But they took a minute to process. It was the most words that I had heard in a long time.

"No. I'd like to hear you speak more. If you're

staying up. It's been so long since I had a real conversation. I thought I might have forgotten how."

"It's possible. But it doesn't sound like it. You sound just fine. In the night though, you did make some funny noises."

His hand reached to my shoulder and his warmth nearly startled me. His hand had that same gentle yet firm combo as his voice. It was a welcome touch. I wanted to see his face but his voice would have to do.

"How long have you been here? I've never seen a man look so exhausted."

I tried to think back. "I don't know. But it's been a long time. Too long. I keep telling myself I'll get used to it. But you never do. We'll never…"

The words left me and I cried, unable to hold back the tears anymore. All the exhaustion, knowing we couldn't be planet-side, it was all too much. His words, a conversation in my native tongue, it brought on waves of homesickness. Hearing my tears he came closer and sat down next to me on the cot.

"You're still you. They can't take that from you. No matter what they do to us they can't take that away. Not from any of us."

"Where do you think they are taking us? The gravity. This place has to be a ship. But where to? Why?"

"Let's not think about that now. Tell me about you. How did you end up here? Who were you before this place?"

"I don't remember anything but waking up in one of these cells." I gestured to the darkness, "None of us do. Do you?"

"No. It's the same for all of us. I meant before this place. The last thing you remember. This might be a prison, but I don't think we're criminals."

The thought had never occurred to me. When one is punished for so long one finds reasons. It was difficult to think back that far, into another life which was so completely gone.

"I...I was a pilot. I was flying. Asteroid mines. Backup and debris control." It was coming back in jagged flashes, a picture show far removed. "But I don't think we were supposed to be there. No one was around, there was a warning beacon. We thought it was too old to have meaning. Maybe we are criminals. I don't know, I don't know anything anymore."

I hadn't thought about these things in so long I had nearly forgotten them. No matter how many times I had been over it I couldn't connect my last memories with arriving here or being captured.

Again, he shushed me. "We don't have to talk about it if it's hard. Tell me anything you want. It's just nice to hear a human voice after all this time."

I couldn't think of anything to say. In my head I had so many names for what we had been doing: mining, company work, salvage. But we had been pirates going out into the universe to suck up every resource we could find. My role was unimportant enough to shift blame and tell myself that it was only a job and that humans had the right. How many species here had been busy telling themselves the same thing?

My friend's comment had been so genuine and unassuming, but my memories brought anger and guilt in an unhealthy mix. Even though I could think of no victim in what we had been doing, possibly no crime at all, it was our mentality that had been wrong. Sometimes we don't know our overindulgence until we can look at it from the lens of having nothing, or less than nothing. And now that I had something, a friend without judgement, I was squandering our brief time together with pointless self-pity for a crime I was unsure of. What had happened before this place didn't matter, it was gone, obliterated. Now was what mattered. It was all we had and I was filling it with confused poisoned memories. So busy thinking that I had missed what he had been saying. Wasting moments of calm that would soon pass into God knows what possible awfulness. Normally mental flights from the cell were welcome fantasy. Now, I needed to get back in that room. His voice filled it and called to me, and I wanted nothing but for it to tether me in, for him to speak to me forever, for his companionship to last. But it wouldn't, couldn't, and my chance would soon pass.

"I'm sorry. I spaced out for a moment. Still haven't quite slept enough."

His face must have been kind with understanding, no anger on it, not even a touch of irritation.

"Yes. That's right. You couldn't have had more than four or five hours. You must be exhausted." I couldn't see his arms but imagined him gesturing for me to lay back down. "And here I am rambling, keeping you up. I'm sorry, you sleep. It's just that I haven't bunked with another human before. There's a few of us here but I've barely been able to exchange words. The other guys are fine, but it's not the same. But you seem sick. And I'm worried about you. I can just watch over you though. I'll keep quiet."

His voice lilted away in the last words. They were earnest but filled with a lonesome distance that called to me. There would be other times to sleep but perhaps never another to spend a night alone together. As he had said, humans are rare here, bunking with one even rarer. My eyes were still heavy but my heart began to flutter and race. In the dark I reached out and touched his face. It was in need of a shave, rough and burly, but beneath his skin was warm and human, oh so human. He reached out, too, and touched my face, his hand as warm as the rest of him. I could only guess at what this touch told him, but he made a small, satisfied sound and moved his hand to stroke the back of my neck. For all the scales, chiton, feathers and other things I had no name for that had comforted me here, that human touch brought with it feelings and memories that no other hand could. It was as if it held a fistful of earth from home. And it intoxicated me. It brought a sense of relief that I couldn't help but want to return.

Sliding off the bunk I moved to the floor in front of him. His hand followed and he began a word he did not finish. My hands on his legs, I pushed them slightly apart and felt for the clasp of his uniform pants, unfastening then pulling gently. He understood and lifted his body slightly to help me as I took them away from his hips and down his legs. His scent intensified and without being able to see I knew that he rose in that moment. I took him into my hand and knew that I was correct. I could feel the beating of his heart pulse through him as I clasped and moved with the timing. His legs tensed and their rigidity pulled me in, locked me in. My free hand moved under his shirt and up past his chest to his face. He took my finger in his mouth as I took him into mine. I could imagine his eyes rolling and knew that they did. I brought my hand back down and moved my fingers under his hips, pulling him toward me and in further. He joined in this lifting, slow at first, then becoming a thrust. Following his movement I pulled him in deeper and deeper inside me and could feel his balls begin to lift. I slowed down to make him want for it and could feel his tension mount. Then I moved back down his member with greater enthusiasm until my lips met the base; I held it there as long as I could before returning to the steady stroke. I knew he was almost there when his hand found the back of my head and moved it to his uncontrollable rhythm. Once more he pushed up with his pelvis and simultaneously down with his hand, and released. He flooded my mouth with the oceans of the Earth. For a moment I stood on high cliffs overlooking the waves as that great body moved with the moon and up and down the shores. His body twitched several more times and relaxed. Letting out a held breath he slowly fell back onto the cot. Breath became a murmur of pleasure.

I crawled up and on top of him, savoring the flavor of Earth and his smell, which was at once both new and familiar. Comforting. I fought the urge to sleep as my hand found his hair and scenes from our planet danced across my mind. I couldn't see his face in the darkness but knew it was a picture of home. In that moment I was desperately torn between never wanting it to end and my unsated exhaustion. The latter won out.

When I awoke, still on top of him, the lights were still mercifully out. The night was not over. And I feared that at any second they would flip on and break this private moment. We would inevitably be taken away and never run into each other again. It had felt so good to speak in full sentences. To be understood and to read expressions with no doubt of what they meant. He too was stirring into wakefulness and rolled like a kitten coming to. I tried not to move, to stretch out the moment, but my tension brought him about.

"Hello you," he whispered.

"Shhh. Kiss me while you still can."

He didn't wait and moved to my mouth. Again, I tasted the Earth on him, so far from this dreadful place, a taste of freedom, one I felt only he could give me. It filled my heart with escape, and in that second I would have killed to flee with him, to find some place where our private moment could last, could continue indefinitely.

The ugly lights returned breaking the revery, but brought his face back to focus; I tried to memorize his features, to connect it with the tenderness of the night. I could think of nothing but him being taken away from me, forever.

When the door to the cell clanked open, they marched us down separate halls and I knew we would probably never encounter each other again. The memory of his face began to recede from me with every echoing footstep. Each step was a hammer on my heart. Each step emphasized the months here. Each step took with it the hope that escape was possible and awaited us in a future together. I tried to make these thoughts steel my resolve to find a way out, not just for me but for all of the men here. It wouldn't work. They brought with them unhappiness. And as much as I wanted to turn and get one last look at him, my fear of recourse from the guards prevented me from fulfilling that urgent desire. They had trained me well and I saved them from the need for their duty as I punished myself by stifling that longing.

All the freedom of the night was gone, barely a memory. It took with it my resolve and my dignity, and when these were gone nothing was left but a shell, miserable and afraid. I would have cut off an arm for the strength to turn and smile at the guard, to riot with abandon. An hour before perhaps I could have. Would have. But now the defiance and earthly freedom was gone and self-pity took over in pathetic acceptance of having lost it so quickly after it had come. The memory of his touch became a cold empty cell and my mind did pointless loops which matched our worthless circles around the rec-room. One more circumnavigation was enough to defeat me. If I wasn't defeated already.

Dejected as I was now, that I had had some rest and yesterday's meal, some sense of normalcy returned, at least for my body. My feet no longer dragged, I had enough strength to run, but my mind was sluggish and struggling to keep a dense depression at bay. The looks on the faces of other inmates told similar stories. Had they been starved and sleep-deprived too, or had the air of the prison completely changed in the last week? Not that the prison had ever been a happy place, but now something about it felt worse. That moment of zero G had probably crushed the hopes of escape for many of the men. And for many the hopes of escape, false or otherwise, were the last bit of hope to cling to.

Dashed in one moment.

The walls here are so close that a man forgets how to see very far. That hope-crushing moment may also have saved many a potential escapee from sucking vacuum. But no one was seeing it that way. A malaise had set in and it sat like an acrid smoke across everything, raising the tension in the men. The guards didn't seem to notice or care, but rather, still wore their endlessly blank non-expressive expressions. I had a bad feeling. The atmosphere in the halls was bad and getting worse. Not a word spoken, but you could just tell. Something was wrong. Or it was going to be.

We were headed to the rec but something was off. The line was moving slower than usual, almost imperceptibly, but when one grows so used to a routine even the slightest deviation sticks out drastically. Something was holding us up ever so slightly. And it was making the men restless. The subtle shift was enough to rouse the men and when the line slowed further the fear crept up on me. I wasn't the only one. I saw muscles bunch in the backs of those in front of me. A dangerous audible murmur. And then the guards were in on the disturbance. Prods went into several backs accompanied by pained grunts, which in turn were met with another jab. But the second strike didn't quiet the line. One man fell to his knees and his amphibious looking body made a soft splat sound when it hit the floor. Most of the men took a step to the right against the wall as we had been trained, and the guards swarmed to the fallen man. But they did not raise him to his feet. They rained blows on him. A horrible sound of metal on flesh. Gasps from the men, those that hadn't turned away from the gruesome sight. But the guards were too preoccupied with the beating to respond to the sound.

They worked harder, setting an example for the rest of us, continuing to harm the man who had done nothing but lose his footing in response to violence. It was unbearable to watch as they laid into him, and his cries grew in volume until it ceased. But the beating continued until he lay there limp and unmoving. Even then they kept at it with their prods until there was nothing left but wet sounds.

More guards entered the hall replacing those who, now finished with their beating, were starting to gather up the man, who, appearing dead, put up no resistance to his removal. We waited in silent fear as they went about their ugly work and when they were done, we were forced to walk through the coagulating puddle of blood left behind. Bloody footprints accompanied us into the next room and when some slipped in the gore the tension further grew, but no guard moved to intervene. They were sending a message, one that no man in the line failed to understand.

It wasn't the first time I had seen a man beaten to death, but it's not a sight one gets used to. His blood formed a circle around the rec, dragged by so many feet, and as it dried it began to stink. Every step led you back to it, so there was no avoiding the loop of carnage. The guards looked on as if nothing had happened. No one looked up to face them, rather staring at the dirty floor in our pointless circling, and I did the same, for all feared meeting the same fate and knew how little provocation it would take to rouse the guards into further violence.

Each loop around the room intensified my anger and everything in me wanted to pull something stupid. They had killed the man for nothing, merely for slowing down. It could have been any of us. I hadn't known him, but he was me, he was all of us, just another nameless convict wondering why he had awakened in this hell.

There was enough of us to take the few guards in the room but the men showed no signs of being ready for revolt. We had been cowed into submission. It hung like a fog in the room. So, we walked and walked, each footfall sticking to the floor and making a grotesque peeling sound when lifted. I listened to that evil music and its rising and falling rhythm with disdain, each beat followed by a mounting panic. Knowing I was not alone in this I tried to stifle the feeling, and I knew every man did the same in that moment. It went on and on. Either they were marching us longer than usual, or the tangible fear stretched out our time into a circle of mounting hate.

Eventually they funneled us out of the increasingly rotten rec-room, this time without social time at the end. On the way out they made each of us pause for a moment to have our feet washed off. The water was like ice and stung in more ways than one. When the last of us were through I could hear them hosing down the room, but the stench would not leave me. It lingered like a phantom.

Arriving at the mess I didn't think I could eat, and the dejected faces around me told a similar story, those that I could read anyway. The silence in the room was dreary and loud, and only then did I realize that everyone sat at the benches staring at the "food" but refusing to eat. I too had involuntarily and inadvertently joined in this silent protest. No one had said a word, yet we had all done the same, either through not being able to stomach eating out of sheer revulsion or as a message to the guards; I could not say why. But there we sat, doing nothing, refusing to eat out of a strange impromptu solidarity with our dead comrade. Part of me thought that we should eat, keep up our strength for what might come next, but I would not break the hunger strike, for if we were to act we needed to act together. And they couldn't force feed us all. Could they?

They left us sitting there in front of the food for way longer than the usual mealtime, perhaps thinking that we would cave and give up the gesture. We didn't. Each of us sat there refusing to even look at the gruel that they claimed was food, no matter how tense things became, refusing to budge. When a guard came and approached a man at my table none of us stirred, not even when he crammed the man's face down into the bowl of slop. And to his credit he lifted his face back up, covered in muck, and didn't even bother to wipe it off but rather faced forward stoically, defying the guard in utter silence. This caused quite a stir with the guards who were both unused to defiance and always got their way. I feared that their latest victim would receive more than just soup in the face, but instead the guards cleared the room, leaving us there in silence. Looking around the room at all of those alien faces I wondered if the time had come. If only there had been a universal language among us, or that our sign could be that specific. Anger and tension were high, that much was clear. But what to do with it?

Someone handed him a rag to wipe his face and still he said nothing. No one did. Our comrade's death moments earlier was still fresh in the minds of everyone. But it felt that something had broken, some invisible line had been crossed and there was no going back to the way things were. We stewed in silence over this, but no cohesive plan formed, no words were spoken, nothing external exchanged. But something had changed, something inside each of us.

The guards were on edge for a reason, enough so to kill and humiliate for the slightest infraction. It signaled a moment that each of us was intuitively aware of. The shift had nothing to do with us inmates, whom they already considered expendable, and everything to do with the prison, something that was making them afraid. A malfunction perhaps. Arriving at a destination? Something had them worked up and I knew that if we could figure out what it was, we could leverage it to our advantage. We could have something to work with besides our numbers and anger. We needed to find a way to be more than just a mob. If we became a mob many of us would surely die. If we became an army...

We outnumbered the guards, at least most of us thought so, but there was no way to organize, at least none that I could think of or communicate. But there had to be a way.

The door slammed back open and twice as many guards as I had ever seen in the mess entered and formed a ring around us. None of us had touched the food. The faces of the guards remained placid, unreadable, but I swore I could sense that they were standing a little straighter than usual. So were my fellow inmates. They were holding themselves with a pride I had never seen in such numbers. I too was sitting up straighter. There was no way that the guards missed it.

Their prods came out and signaled a clear message. In silence and with no change of expression the men stood tall and formed a line, this time flanked with guards on either side of us. The untouched food remained on the tables as they marched us out. The hall had been cleaned but the stench of death did not leave us. It was palpable. It mingled with a new atmosphere that all could feel as they returned us to the cells two by two. I watched the men in front of me in the line enter their respective cells, heads held high in self-respect. They had killed one of ours but somehow in that action had killed a fear in us. Some threshold had been crossed, and not just that of our cells. As the prod informed me that we had reached my cell for the night I thought I could sense the guard's fear through his instrument. It felt like I had the better of an armed man, even as defenseless as I was.

There was too much adrenaline pumping through me to calm down and sit. Several minutes went by before I could even focus enough to acknowledge my cellmate. He was small and lay in repose upon his cot. Mostly hair, or fur, it was difficult to see any definition in his physique, but his demeanor was pleasant and his air of calm was in stark contrast to what was happening on the other side of the wall. He gestured for me to sit across from him, but I shook my head in refusal. I still needed time to cool off. My body tensed in anticipation of a riot; now that tension could find no release but to cycle around my insides. Is one ever ready for something like a riot, or is it always a spontaneous act of passion, much like sex with a stranger? Regardless of the answer it was pumping through me, so much so that I had barely noticed that the cold inside the cell had been cranked up. It only came to my attention when I saw the breath leaving me in lazy swirling clouds. The sight sobered me slightly. For eventually the nerves would dissipate and the cold would catch up with me. Hopefully my furry friend would fare better, as the friendly look on his face suggested.

So far he hadn't spoken and when my attention turned to him I tried out a list of various common words that were often understood across multiple species. He shook his head in response and said nothing in return. I followed with various common sign gestures, but these were met with the same lack of response. Perhaps he was a new arrival? But that thought was quickly shattered as an image of the man who had been killed flashed in my mind. It was not the tattered remains I had seen in the hallway, it was him alive and well, as happy as one could be in captivity. He was in a cell no different from this one, sitting on the bunk across from me, translucent blue skin glistening erotically in the fading light. This I saw through the eyes of my current bunkmate, vivid as if it was happening now. With the image came waves of feelings. There was joy and eroticism mixed with lament for what had happened in the hallway. And I knew that he was sharing with me scenes from their intimate encounter the night before. The sensations swept through my being, taking with it the pent-up stress from our near riot and moment of defiance.

All that became irrelevant and I entered their sex through my cellmate's mind. Deep soft skin mingling with downy fur. Caresses which may have never known each other outside of this place. The meeting of their bodies was colored with intermingling slideshows of landscapes. Lovely riparian valleys. Slightly wooded chaparral. Skies of various hues. And bouquets of scent from wild and cultivated plants on their respective planets. Their physical partnership had brought with it an exchange of happier memories, an exchange of the past through physical touch, and now that moment was being shared with me as if in real-time. As these tapestries unfolded in my mind my cellmate approached me, sat down on the bunk close enough that our bodies touched side by side, and when that contact was made the mind images went nova and bloomed into full sensory detail. My body responded to the imagery as if I had been there and involved. Both of their touches were as real as can be and somehow responded to my responses. They worked with my senses as if we'd been lovers for years, knew my every desire and how to fulfill it, they even knew the little idiosyncratic things that I don't like and avoided these. It was almost too much. And when I thought that, they pulled back ever so slightly, making it not only tolerable, but more pleasurable than before.

I opened my eyes, almost surprised to be in the cell sitting on the bunk next to the furry one, and when I looked at him, he just nodded a reassuring nod and brought his hand to my face to close my eyes again. As soon as they were closed, I was back in the throes of their pleasure, our pleasure. The tactile sensations were so vivid as to be indistinguishable from the real thing. The contrast of fur and pliant amphibian skin was exhilarating in a way that is difficult to explain, a mix of textures apparent, but delicate and strange in the most satisfying way. I lost track of who was who, even who I was, as the three of us roiled in an ecstasy I hadn't imagined possible in confinement such as ours. Was I making love to a man's ghost? No. He was here in the flesh, rather in the flesh of my mind. As real as anything. And I knew that even though the man had died, he lived on through my cellmate, and that somehow I would too because of the sharing. At these thoughts the sex gently receded to a memory and my cellmate touched my shoulder to rouse me, then held my hand as we shared in the afterglow in the darkness of the cell.

I'd heard tales of telepaths but had never met one, or really believed. Somehow, I had thought it would merely be an exchange of words from mind to mind, like silent conversation. What we had shared was much more than that. It was an unimaginable gift, one that not only brought us closer than I had thought possible, but also made me one with the man who had been killed in the hallway. That attack had been an affront to us all. More than the death of just one man. But knowing this brought no hatred. Rather it brought a sense of deep impending freedom. A freedom that no prison could shackle. I didn't need to see my cellmate's face to know that the gift he had given was intentional and rare. But the lights clicked on in that moment and his beatific face exuded a knowing kindness. He squeezed my hand tenderly and then slowly got up and returned to his cot as the guards rushed in to separate us.

I wanted nothing but to stay with him and somehow knew that no amount of distance or walls or isolation could really keep us apart. The sharing left something permanent behind in his wake. So much so that I barely noticed the guards as they marched us away from each other. I wondered how many of the men here were aware of his power. The guards seemed to take no notice and were all business as usual. They couldn't know that captivity was meaningless in the face of love, for they had no love in them. Without it they were cut off from the grandeur of the cosmos. It made me pity them for they could never feel the deep sense of connection that I now had with all things. They were nothing. They were small in the face of it. And I knew that it was only a matter of time before their walls crumbled around them into the meaninglessness that their system of punishment really was.

A thwack from a prod against my thigh ended my revelry but could not kill the hope that had risen in me. Whether from my posture or attempt not to flinch he must have sensed a change in my demeanor and added more blows in quick succession for good measure. One to the same spot on my leg, the other to the small of my back. The second made me stagger but I dared not let it fell me for fear of a fatal beating. I winced and kept the pain inside, for later use if needed.

Sated, he prodded me forward but did not hit me again. It was challenging not to try and steal another glance at my friend. Looking straight ahead, so as not to provoke the guard further, I saw other men flogged. Our captors were out to prove some gruesome point. Violence was a language that all understood but I saw no man go down, instead they were attempting to take it stoically.

Last night's death was still fresh in everyone's minds. The guards were out for blood, and while it showed in several places, the prisoners would not comply by showing their pain. I wondered if my friend was being similarly beaten and what would happen if he was touched by someone in hostility. Could intimate sharing occur involuntarily? And how would the guards react if it did spill through their mindset? The thought was terrifying, but I pushed it aside to focus on the moment, hoping to stave off further injury.

They marched us down one hall after another, passing by the rec and the mess without pause. So, we were to be taken elsewhere. This further alteration in the ingrained routine was unsettling. More proof that something was afoot and to be feared. But I wasn't afraid and by the stern looks of my fellow inmates I knew that they were not either, or at the very least doing a good job of containing their terror for the sake of the guards. A small and silent rebellion taking hold. But this sense of victory and impending action slammed shut along with the cell doors as they threw us into new cages, the whole exercise to separate us from the bunkmates with which we had spent the previous night. Although night and day had been made meaningless by the interruptions in schedule and random intervals of light and darkness.

At first, I thought I was the sole occupant of the cell, that they might be rearranging us so that we all faced solitude. Then I saw him. On the floor at the foot of the cot was a bronze puddle. He was one of the few non-bipedal species in the prison. Non-pedal rather. Although I had seen him several times in passing, he remained a mystery. At the moment I wanted to communicate what I felt was beginning to occur, but I had no idea where to start with him. For he had no discernable mouth or limb, and when I looked at him a blurry distorted reflection of myself stared back.

First, I attempted a sign of greeting, but it was met with silence and no gesture. Then I spoke, a simple "hello, my friend," and still silence was returned. Next, I knelt by his side and going out on a limb I reached to him and slowly placed a palm onto his shiny ripple of a body. He recoiled at first and then moved forward to envelope my hand. His touch was at once both warm and cold. Liquid and solid at the same time. He drove farther up my arm and absorbed me up to the wrist. At the same time an unthreatening comfort permeated the places where he touched me. It was a language in and of itself, conveying abstract emotion with an accuracy spoken language is incapable of. I wanted to cry for the purity of it. Tactile and filled with pure feeling. A tear of joy fell. I held out another hand and he enveloped that as well. Never had I thought it possible to convey so much of oneself through simple touch. Who he was, how he felt about the world, and this place – all were present in that touch. How much he could tell about me I couldn't tell, but I got the feeling that the ex-change was mutual, although whatever I was communi-cating must have been crude and rudimentary compared to what his language was capable of. It made me want to immerse myself in him and as I realized this his touch warmed. And the lights went off again.

Slowly backing away I moved to the cot, feeling my way through the darkness with my feet. I tried to imagine experiencing the world solely through touch and what kind of worldview it would lead to, but view wasn't the right word for it. So I tried to stop thinking with my eyes. The cold metal post announced the cot and I settled my body onto it, reclining. He flowed up the post and found my feet. He took them in as much as he had done with my hands and again the conflicting mix of sensations somehow led to a pleasurable feeling.

Then he snaked around my legs, one by one circling them, covering the skin and then leaving them bare, his warmth mixing with the cold of the cell in alternating patterns. He sped up and slowed down conversely, matching the various rhythms of my body, matching it in ways I had never thought possible. Beneath my pants he worked his way up, eventually finding my midsection, but rather than focusing on my crotch like so many lovers would have, he took in the whole area but didn't remain still. He flowed all over me, taking in, letting out, applying slight pressure and releasing at all the right times.

We lacked all other forms of conveying, but his movement and grace were beautifully attentive. I hadn't even known that so many places could produce such pleasure if touched correctly. It was more than being held, it was a return to the aquatic womb from which all life began. He encompassed all of my feelings into that touch and I could only hope that it derived pleasure for him as well, for until then I had not known that touch was capable of such depth, and certainly did not know how to wield it myself. I had no idea how to return, to reciprocate the feelings he produced in me. The orgasm was total, non-localized, spread completely through my body and mind. He rippled, vibrated, a liquid shudder as I came, a movement I could only interpret as mutual pleasure.

For a moment he stayed wrapped around me and then flowed to his cot leaving me quivering in the cold but feeling so warm inside. I would have wanted him to stay in the cot with me. But how does one hold onto a liquid? I had been a complete novice and relied solely on him, unable to give back as I would have liked. Perhaps I was thinking too much like a primate. I would have drunken him in if I could have.

Still not knowing what senses he possessed I said, "Thank you," and I meant it, for he had shown me that the meaning of caring was much vaster than I could have imagined. Humanity wasn't something reserved for humans, which I had known but perhaps not to the extent to which it is true. I had found it here in these cells. Perhaps it was what our captors were in search of? Perhaps it was what the guards wanted to destroy in us? But now I knew that we would never allow that. I could feel all of the men in the prison, finding kindness in their own ways, being shown new ways to love, and finding freedom together no matter what the conditions.

I dreamt of Earth and woke up unsettled and confused by my surroundings. The fog of sleep quickly wore off as the familiar prison walls came into focus, same as they ever were but now feeling too small to hold me in. The lights came on soon after and reflected off of my friend like dazzling ripples in a stream. Why would you imprison such a beautiful creature, such a beautiful man? But it no longer mattered why any of us were put here. Prison, like freedom, is an abstract state of mind. No one could truly take away the things that my friends here had shown me. Our captors most likely could not even define what a man is. I myself was still finding out, and how could they take away that which they did not know existed? No prod can touch our minds. Death could not even steal these men away, for those that had imprisoned us could never contain that which is within us. It didn't matter why we were here, because here is always wherever you find yourself in that moment.

Touching my bronze friend brought back a wave of tender feelings, a sensation that traveled two ways. Never had a last touch felt so permanent, not a separation but a solidarity that could not be broken. Not even when the door creaked open and the guards shouted for us to get up and move. My friend flowed out of the cot and toward the door and I knew I would not need to miss him because he was now just as much a part of me as everyone else.

There were still more guards in the hallway than usual but not nearly as many as the day before. So they were still afraid but also feeling as though they had dispelled the unrest. The prisoners were also calmer. But I noticed that they still stood straighter and moved with pride even though obeying orders. For a moment I thought that they would merely shuffle us off to different cells again but it soon became apparent that they were moving us back into the regular prison routines, as if nothing had happened. As if a day or two was enough to obliterate the cruelty which we had seen. They must have suspected that they had instilled the fear in us once again. But they knew nothing about us. We were one entity, but it was a mistake to think that we could be moved as one through punishments which now struck me as irrelevant. They could kill me, or others, and it would not change a thing. They couldn't build a prison big enough to contain the richness that was really hidden within these walls. So, I stood taller with the others as I was led down the halls and back to the same old rec, which in my mind was not a punishment of tedium but rather a circle of life. The guards did not need to walk the circle to be trapped within it, that cycle was one that none of them could escape. It was a matter of how you moved through it. And I could even find beauty in the simple act of stretching my legs after days in the cells. I found that I even looked forward to the social time, if there was to be one, and to the poor excuse for food. With a mind so alive my body followed suit and craved every sensation, all being equally valid and worthwhile. Though many of the faces in the circle were virtually unreadable I thought I saw in them something new, something shared, and it was more than defiance, so much more. I saw in the men the expression of the cosmos in all of its glorious variety, an experiment which moved toward an elusive perfection, never quite getting there but always moving closer.

And they walked us and they walked us, way longer than usual. When the tedium of the circling caught up to me, my mood of liberty began to shrink. Faces were now long and footsteps dragged. They were trying to wear us out, to exhaust us. For some of the men it appeared to be working. Either they were trying to keep us down by forcing us to be too tired to act, or it was some new form of mundane punishment, or both. At first, I had lost track of time while in my thoughts but when I started to feel it in my legs I began counting the circles. We must have been at it for hours. My legs screamed at me to stop. Then I knew. They were waiting for one of us to collapse, so an example could be set. And as tired as some of the men looked, they refused to go down.

The man walking in front of me, and his back, became more and more desirable places to lean, and I imagined the man behind me felt much the same way. I could also see it in the eyes of the men across the circle. One of them stumbled, tripping over his own feet. The tension in the room rose and the silence became even deeper, a hush which rode every single one of us, fearful of what response might come if someone were to cry out. Those looks of pride I had seen earlier were disappearing one by one. The guards' game of attrition was beginning to work and it burst my heart into flames to see it happening right in front of me, happening to me as well. We did the only thing we could do: we walked the circle refusing to fall, refusing to give them what they wanted.

I wanted to shout to the men that we could beat them at this if we didn't give up. But the cry would be viewed no differently than a fall in the eyes of the guards. If someone did fall, would they make us circle in the blood as they had before? Picturing it in my mind I imagined that if they did it would throw the men into action. A breaking point. But this thought was cracked in half at the sudden call to reenter the hall. So the violence was to be delayed for the threat of it. There would be no social period. The latter was to be expected but I was shocked that they had avoided the beatings they seemed so eager to engage in. The relief was thick in the air and no man dared let his gait falter even though everyone's legs had to have grown as weary as mine.

Exhaustion was near total. The sounds of heavy breathing surrounded us. Perhaps they preferred any violence to take place in the halls rather than the circle. Perhaps it was easier to clean up the blood in confined spaces. My mind would not let the potential of violence go. I imagined that these same thoughts circled through the mind of every prisoner. Pictures of my amphibian friend flashed through my vision. Not of his death, but of his life. A beautiful life that had been taken away only because he had slowed in his movement as I so wanted to do now.

Our captors probably never considered his life, or any of ours for that matter. What they had stolen from each of us meant nothing to them, taken away completely for some unknown motivation that probably meant a fate worse than death. I no longer cared why. Thoughts of taking back our freedom pushed all others aside and I was sure that these thoughts were to become a psychic cloud that would envelop us all. Through our enforced march we were becoming one single entity. One which had been forced into a position where there was nothing left to lose.

Instead of throwing us back in the cells again our march ended at the mess. Stomachs and mouths grumbled with relief as it had been too long since any of us had eaten. Fortunately, the walking punishment had not left any of us in a striking mood. We moved to our designated seats as the guards formed a ring around the room. For a moment I put myself in their shoes, the sheer boredom of power, a boredom which would probably lead to more violence. But I turned my empathy off. Today was not the time for that, not of all days.

One by one the men got up and went to the slot for their tray of calories. Many of them groaned when standing up, overwhelmed with fatigue and too starving to refuse to get up and eat. When my turn came my body roiled in protest, but my stomach won the argument and forced me to the slot. Much as earlier I imagined that most of the men here were running through similar internal dialogs. I could almost hear it. And all the while the guards loomed in the background, staring hard stares, waiting for their moment.

When I sat back down, I had to stop myself from devouring the food too quickly and losing it from a revolting stomach that was tender from neglect. But each bite was welcome and with each I could feel my spirit and energy return. From the sounds in the room I could tell that I wasn't alone in the relief pumping through my body. As I looked around I saw men, again sitting up straighter, the feelings of defiance returning, and also I saw friends. Friends from many nights past. People I had shared discreet chunks of my life with and had never been able to have a follow up conversation with. The people who had made life bearable during my time here, all sharing in our predicament and all sharing what little love we had left. Love that was enough to fill a prison the moment the guards looked away. And now I saw that look on many of the faces right in front of the leering guards. None cared to hide it anymore and stole sideways flirty looks with one another. There was enough of this that the guards began to take notice and started shifting from foot to foot, unsure of what it meant. But no words had been exchanged, so no rules had been broken.

Fear and love mixed in the air, clashing and attempting to undo each other. The strongest of emotions in a game of tug-of-war. For a moment, immersed in mixed emotions, I thought about what it would be like to fuck one of the guards and share something more than confined space. I even chose one by looking at his posture, but as I scanned the room I saw my furry psychic friend. He was sitting quietly, unmoving, an island of peace in the room. And he did something that brought all eyes to him.

He stood up on his chair and then moved up to the table, an act of sheer defiance, a shattering of the rules, now towering over us all. It was so unexpected that the guards even froze for a moment. Before they could act he sent out a radiant burst into the minds of all of us there, even the guards, who responded with stunned blankness. In that moment we all shared in each other's lives and loves, our fears and pain. And at the forefront of it all, a plan.

In unison we rose from the benches, all standing tall with a new flush of energy. He raised his furry arms to the ceiling and a single word found its way to each of our minds, "Now."

In a split second everyone was on their feet. The guards who had formed a ring around the mess had nowhere to go, except the few by the door to the hall. The men went for those first. They were subdued and dragged back into the room before inmates blocked the exit completely with a bench torn from the ground.

Cries of pain filled the room as prods made contact with flesh, and the air filled with the smell of burning since some of them had been turned up to amplify the pain of the strike. Against this came a wave of blows from meal trays and every type of limb imaginable. Time slowed as I wielded my tray and made my way through the chaos toward the closest guard. He was the same I had fantasized about, but now my purpose was singular.

Bringing the tray up in an arc it struck his chin, offsetting his footing slightly. He returned a blow with his prod, clipping my shoulder in searing fire. I pushed the pain aside and continued with the tray until he was down men swarmed in to shower him with kicks. I heard the wet sound of a foot to the stomach and then it was quiet again.

It couldn't have lasted more than a minute and all the guards were down. Many of the inmates were now armed with prods and others wearing the guards' helmets. We had outnumbered them, but it ended so quickly, almost as if it had never happened. There was a cheer as the realization spread that no guard was left standing in the mess, followed by a moment of confusion as it dawned on us that few had thought past this small victory.

Again, my friend raised himself to the table, and placid as ever connected our thoughts into something purposeful. I was overjoyed that he was uninjured. Very few of us were hurt in the guards' inefficient attempt to quell what had merely been a riot but was now a rebellion. As this distinction spread from one mind to another, we tore the makeshift barricade from the door and spilled out into the hall.

Guards were already beginning to flood in from the other end and were made quick work of in such tight quarters. With each that fell we gained an armed prisoner. With each that fell the excitement grew and increased our vigor.

We marched down the halls clearing one after another, checking the cells as we went, making sure not to leave any man behind. The place was a labyrinth of repetition and I might have thought we were going around in circles if it wasn't for the fresh waves of guards that kept pouring in. But so too did our ranks grow as we cleared one room after another. We were sheer inertia as we used our numbers like a blade, cutting through the prison and sacking our captors one after another.

The halls might have grown congested if we were not so used to the march and linked through a thread of the mind. Men were freed from solitary holes as we moved, joining in as they were emancipated one by one. More and more of us armed as we went. I still wielded a tray as if I had been training with one and brought it crashing down on every helmeted head that came upon me. As bodies fell they were left where they lay in the relentless push forward. Ours were also among them and in our minds we felt them leaving us while at the same time becoming a part of us forever. Their pain only added to our calculated rage, their energy joining ours in a wave of blows, strengthening our advance.

The sounds of men rose like sex. We were an intimate body, one in our pent-up violence. All those years stolen from us coming together in a singular cry for freedom. But even though each of us was intertwined with the rapture of violence I never saw any of the men overdo it. Guards fell one by one, but the inmates did not go for overkill as the guards had whenever using their show of violence as a tool to keep us in line. The guards were merely oppressors which were in the way of freedom and needed to be quickly disposed of. Fortunately, for many, the anger had not fermented into hate. Mine may have, if it wasn't for their company in the nights, and now those men, warriors out of necessity, were glorious in battle. I wished I could leave the melee and be a spectator, if only to see that clash of bodies in valorous action, men with nothing to lose and everything to gain, lives on the line but so much more, freedom, but not merely for any individual, for all. I knew that even if I fell I would not be left behind, and that if I were to die in that very moment I would not be forgotten.

The triumph in my mind exploded into pieces as pain shot through my back. It was at once both blunt force and the cracking sting of electricity. A prod. It brought me to my knees but unseen hands lifted me from the shoulders, and as they did I brought the tray up and, smashing into the chin of my assailant, I took his prod and left him there.

The throng flowed on, taking me with it. It was a blur of fighting. Grunts. Blows. Sizzling of electricity. Shouts of battle – the chaos in the air unified our intent. The men were an unstoppable force, and now, mostly armed, cut through the remaining guards with grace and speed.

The halls grew less noisy as we went. Here and there a clatter would emerge as another guard was taken care of, until even this stopped. Then heavy breathing was the only sound. We looked around at each other hardly believing that the assault was over. No one dared cry out in victory though. For we were still confined in familiar halls. Stoically we marched to the door to which we had always been denied access. Heat dissipated from our heaving backs as we prepared ourselves for what might be on the other side.

We made quick work of the door with our prods and brought it crashing down with a thud that rang out in the near silence of the prison. Slowly the men entered, one by one, into a huge, cavernous room dimly lit in the glowing light of electronics. The walls were lined with row upon row of mostly empty chambers. A few still contained inert bodies of deactivated guards, lifeless in their charging stations.

In the center of the room were more rows containing stacks of housing for some monstrosities of computation. So, this was our captor. No organic mastermind of punishment but merely a computer left behind by some evil to run the show of our imprisonment.

This impersonal tyrant, the face which we had

sought and did not exist, was reduced to rubble in a matter of minutes. Our impromptu wrecking crew brought the machine down into a pile of useless trash. And then the cheers rose as the remaining lifeless bodies of the shelved guards were taken to pieces.

The shouts of victory became a tumult as the dancing began to the music of ecstatic cries. The men embraced, drew each other near, friends of the night were reunited and brothers made of those who had never spoken until that glorious moment. I kissed strangers and lovers alike as we trampled the wrecked machines of captivity underfoot.

A hush came over the crowd as it instinctively parted to let through the small furry man who had begun our revolt with his warm clarion call of love and freedom. He moved slowly through the rows of men, making eye contact with each and sharing all that he was and could be psychically with the group as a whole. I had never felt so much love radiate through so many at once, especially not in this place. Nods of agreement followed him as he went.

When he reached the far end of the massive room, he stood motionless for a moment at the base of the huge black steel wall. His hands deftly worked the panel there and without a sound the wall raised itself into the ceiling to reveal the first window I had seen in years. Outside the glory of the stars shone onto us, framed by the close horizon of a bright gray asteroid, confirming our suspicions that the prison was a ship. But also so much more, a miniature planetoid of our own, hurtling through space, free.

We had no idea of our destination, and in that moment it didn't matter. The prison was ours. But it was no longer a prison. It was now our home. Tears flowed. Forgotten smiles found their way to faces. And an awed silence blanketed the men as they looked out into the endless open of space.

I moved forward, hardly able to contain my grin as tears spilled into it. I thought of our amphibian friend who had paid the price for all of us. By the window I took my friend's hand in mine, drawing him closer in.

And in the light of a million stars, in a room full of friends, we kissed as free men.

END

THE ORCHARDMAN

By Peter Schutes

OUTBREAK

The floor is made of stones that were broken, cemented together with shiny white concrete, then polished flat. They reflect the cruel, harsh white lights, something a dirt floor back home could never do. For just a few days, we get the softest mattresses and the nicest showers. The maids clean up after us. But it's not really for us orchardmen; it's for the leaders, or helmsmen, whose money built this secret federal hospital; it's more like a prison than a place of healing. The soft mattress and the nice shower are for them. The amenities were built for their comfort while lying with us, but they also serve to ease their conscience in light of what they've done to our people. They only see what they want. They never see where we go after the seed is planted; we get moved back to the dormitory, or "chicken coop," as we call it, to gestate with the other orchardmen. It's a monotonous Hell, punctuated with cycles of conception, gestation, and painful birth.

My name is Shepard Hendrix, and I am one hundred percent full-blooded Monachee. Before the sickness, most folks outside the area of Goochland, Virginia had never heard of of the Monachee race. We lived way back in the hills and only a few of us ever went to grammar school. We boys were mostly home-schooled by our fathers and the girls got their learnings from their mothers. When the population crisis started, we didn't notice. Then we started hearing how nobody down in Goochland was having any babies. It had been three years, and not a single infant was born. Meanwhile, up on Hendrix Hill, we all were popping out babies like usual.

My Pa, Boone Hendrix, subscribed to the Richmond newspaper. We didn't have any TV. He was the first one to tell us about the plague in Africa. It started somewhere in the middle and spread like the common cold. It didn't have any noticeable symptoms other than a scratchy throat and maybe some sneezes. After a man would catch it, he carried it and spread it, and his sperm count dropped, but nothing else happened. Women, however, became barren. The thing was, it spread throughout the whole world before anyone really figured out what was happening. It was so contagious you could get it from being in the same room as a carrier.

We Monachee were immune because of our different reproductive systems. Suddenly, people stopped pretending we weren't in the same store as them. They noticed us. We came to town with a couple of babies on our backs, and the whole town would stare at us in envy. AT the grocery store, the women would beg to hold our babies and softly cry before handing them back. It was nice to be noticed for a change. We weren't ignorant, but we thought the best of people. It turns out we should have stayed home and thought the worst. Because mere weeks later, the government declared martial law. Then the feds built the chicken coops, herded up all the Monachee in Appalachia and beyond, and now here I sit.

I've lived in this secret federal Monachee male facility for six years now as an orchardman. Orchardmen are child-bearers. Seedsmen are Monachee who fertilize the orchardmen. The helmsmen don't like to admit that they've stopped producing sperm, so they always have their way with us first. The seedsmen step in after. My sisters and aunts are hopefully still alive, kept somewhere else. My brother isn't here either. We can't leave, and we are here for one reason only: to produce male babies for the wealthy helmsmen.

Monachee men can only carry male babies, and the women can only have females. By tradition, a Monachee man comes of child-bearing age at eighteen. He may choose to marry a woman, of course, but he's gotta pop out a boy, or we get out of balance. In the Monachee tradition, my Pa got me pregnant shortly after my eighteenth birthday. I was so excited for it. There's no way to feel closer in Monachee society. Babymaking is what sons and fathers do best together. It might sound taboo to normal folks, but it's how things work in our society. Or how they worked before all this.

I'm not going to tell you it was easy; it hurt like hell! Like most Monachee men, Pa's longer than a ruler and thick as a can of beer. It's gotta be real long to plant the seed deep enough. But I wish it didn't have to be so damn thick. My folks told me it's to prepare us for childbirth. My brother Junior is longer and thicker than our Pa. Me, I'm the biggest in the family. It's down to my knee and thick as a big can of tomato sauce. It's on account of my size that they classified me as an orchardman and not a seedsman. That means I gotta carry babies, but I don't have to plant any. It's easier than being a seedsman who spends every working day impregnating other Monachee men, and all the while, he has to carry a baby inside him, too. No womb goes to waste in a world with a shortage of babies.

The seedsmen are taken regularly in a bus with no windows to the hospital prisons where my aunts and sisters are probably kept. Monachee women, after coupling with a Monachee man, make pureblood girl babies that are immune to the plague. I heard that during the ceremony, the girls occasionally get pregnant with helmsmen's babies and bear a daughter who will succumb to the plague. It's cruel, but she will have her rich daddy's blood, which isn't worth a damn, but it matters to them. Those daughters, in a dozen years, will be adoptive mothers to our children. They won't have to stain their insides with seed. They call them "Immaculates."

I'm 25 years old. I've given birth to one baby from my father and seven more from strangers. My son, the one I made with my father, was taken by the adoption squad not long after he came into this world. He's seven years old now, living with a rich family somewhere far from here. I can't say I think I'll ever see him again. Like I said, my brother, Junior, went to another facility. I miss him awful bad. We got separated because the helmsmen, like slave owners before them, knew they could control us better if they kept our families apart. This destruction of our families made the whole baby-making operation run smoother. It's a lot easier to get a man to submit to sex when he's alone and demoralized. Family gets in the way of the factory's mission to repopulate Earth with fertile women and Monachee men.

The ritual is rape with a polite name. I don't have much choice, but I enjoy it. I don't like to let on that I like having sex. If it wasn't for the natural enjoyment God put in our backsides for us, I'd probably have succumbed to depression or worse. But I secretly enjoy the ritual, no matter who's doing it.

To begin the ritual, a helmsman enters, followed by a Monachee seedsman with a long, slender cock. I am required to address the helmsman as Sir. I must begin every ritual with a deep bow and address the helmsman, "I will carry the fruit. You plant the seed." It's bullshit because the helmsmen are all sterile. The seedsman politely waits while the helmsman fucks me on the soft mattress. I haven't met a helmsman yet who has a dick big enough to knock me up. Compared to a seedsman, the helmsman with his little cock is a walk in the park. It doesn't hurt one bit. The seedsman jumps in after the helmsman leaves his infertile seed in me. The seedsman supposedly "pushes" the seed up inside me so the helmsman can pretend his sperm was strong enough to fertilize me. Everyone knows the Monachee seedsman plants the viable seed when he finishes. Monachee women can conceive from a helmsman if the plague hasn't left him entirely infertile. With us men, the sperm has to land deep in the guts, or else it's too weak by the time it gets there. A few seconds makes all the difference.

It's been two weeks since I had my latest child ripped from my breast. Tonight, I'm going through my eighth ritual. Whoever is keeping us prisoner here doesn't care to tell us names or anything in advance. There's a buzz, and then a seedsman escorts a helmsman into the fancy room. Wham bam, thank you, man, and it's done. At least, that's the script.

2

A HELMSMAN

Tonight's ritual was different. Just before 8:00 pm, I stripped down to my birthday suit. Most men don't want to see my cock, so I stuffed it into a king-size pillowcase. The door buzzed, and two men entered. The seedsman was new. He had oily black hair that hung in delicate curls around a pair of midnight blue eyes set in a face that belonged on TV. I knew he was a Seedsman not only because he wore prison orange and had dusky skin but because of the big hump on his back that every Monachee man has. He stood where I could see him and stroked himself to get ready. I couldn't take my eyes off him.

I bowed to the helmsman and said, "I will carry the fruit," but he waved me off. As was the tradition, he stood so he could penetrate me through a hole in the curtain. A typical rich helmsman, concerned with class distinctions, or so I thought. When the ritual got underway, he was a total surprise. He stepped out from behind the curtain. He put his nose in my butt and licked my ass! It felt so good. He did it better than my Dad. He yanked off the pillowcase and stroked my cock.

"Holy shit! You're huge!" He admired my thick hose, stroking it like a farmer admiring his prize bull.

I risked a beating and spoke. "Your kid will be huge, too."

"Maybe. He might only get mine."

I chuckled silently to myself. All the helmsmen want to believe that the seedsman is nothing more than a sperm plow that magically makes us conceive from their loins. Unless the helmsman is hung like a Monachee, those weak swimmers are dead on arrival if they ever were to arrive so deep in the first place. The Monachee seedsman is always the real father.

It had been nine years since I lay with my Pa. The seedsmen were selected for their narrow cocks. It was less bloody and way more efficient. I wasn't prepared when the helmsman penetrated me. He was nearly as thick as Pa, and his cock was abnormally long for a regular man. It was so long my hole wasn't prepared as he pushed past that second hole.

"I'm sorry. Did I hurt you?" The helmsman put a comforting hand on my shoulder.

"No, it's just you're so thick! I'm okay."

I wasn't exactly okay. With each thrust, I grunted with pain, but it was the good kind. I was used to long, narrow cocks and the normal tiny dicks that helmsmen usually sported. The helmsman's was like a slightly shorter version of Pa. Pa. He had been an orchardman here, too. I only ever saw him for a few minutes in the cafeteria or out in the yard. He lived in a different wing of the hospital before he got moved somewhere else, or so they told me. I missed him, and this reminded me of him. I held back tears.

The helmsman was talented. I felt him pop through the curve, repeating it a hundred times. I was a quivering mess. I had to see who this was who was making me orgasm without even touching myself.

I broke every rule in Monachee prison and stole a glance at the man making love to my insides.

He was an old guy in his fifties but still handsome.

He might have been a politician before the plague and martial law. Now, he was just an extremely gifted love-maker. He saw me and grinned, then entered deep inside me.

"Willing to break the rules. I like that. How about you, Jedediah? You like to break the rules?"

The handsome seedsman nodded.

"Well, go on then."

Jed lowered his pants. He was Monachee. He was long like a donkey but not as thick. In one swift movement, he held my chin and put his meat in my mouth. I had never done that. It was punishable by death. When he kept pushing, I gagged and coughed. He held my head and gently pressed past the back of my mouth down my throat. I couldn't breathe, and I felt like I was gonna puke, but it was new and exciting.

Jedediah said, "You got a pretty mouth, man."

I coughed again, and he withdrew partway so I could breathe and stop gagging. We were doing homo stuff. They killed all the homos they could find, accusing them of unnatural acts that didn't lead to childbirth. I'm pretty sure I've got no baby-making equipment in my gullet, so this simple, pleasurable moment was flirting with death. A seedsman wasting his sperm in my mouth!

Jedediah forced his way back down my throat. It felt good to be used like that. Jed locked eyes with the helmsman, and they kissed above me. I was scared someone would come in and send us all to hang. But it just kept going.

Jed made ten or twenty deep thrusts at a time, giving me a few seconds to breathe in between. I caught a glance in the mirror; I could see the outline of Jedediah's cock as it snaked past my Adam's apple.

"Oh, that is so damn hot." The helmsman was close. "I want to say your name when I come. Will you say mine?"

"Mmm"

"I'll wait until Jedediah finishes."

Jed held my nose to his crotch. "Aaah, fuuuuck." Suddenly, in a rush, Jedediah wasted his seed in my throat. I swallowed, afraid it would get me killed. I could feel warm rivers flowing down my gullet. He pulled out the whole length and sprayed my face with the last of his load. The helmsman licked my cummy lips and face clean.

"I'm Daniel St. John. And you?"

"Shepard. Shepard Hendrix, sir."

He said, "Hendrix? You're a Hendrix?"

"Yes, sir."

Daniel said, "Say my name."

"Daniel St. John."

Daniel was in heaven. So was I. He pounded my ass like an auto mechanic fixing a drive shaft. He hammered, twisted, and rotated. I was drooling clear pre-cum on the mattress.

"Shepard! Shepard! I'm gonna make a baby in you! It's coming!"

"Fuck me, Daniel. Make me pregnant!" I'd said it before, but I had never meant it or believed it possible. This horse-hung Daddy was going to knock me up.

"Oh yeah! Shepard! Yeah!" I felt his release way up in the colon. He grabbed my hard cock and jerked it. I was so close that the shock of his touch put me over.

"Oh God, Daniel, you make me feel so good!" It was no lie. My cock boiled over. I made a map of France on the mattress. Daniel broke the law when he reached under and wet his fingers, tasting my seed.

"Shepard Hendrix, thank you. Remember my name, will you?"

"Yes, sir, I'll bear your fruit, sir."

Again, he waved his hands to shut me up. He leaned in and gave a conspiratorial whisper. "Hendrix, that's an important name. Royal Monachee."

I'd heard something like that from Daddy. Like we came from kings. We sure didn't used to live like kings, and we weren't kings of anything now.

Daniel added, "I mean it. Remember my name. You're gonna need it."

I turned to Jedediah, expecting him to have me next. He shook his head and smiled. He was all zipped up.

My heart sank as I watched them go. I was tired, but I had made a mess of my blanket. The maids don't do blankets. I didn't care - I would only be here a few days until the test results came in. If they're negative, I would have to go through another rape. If, by some miracle, this helmsman had impregnated me, I would move back to the chicken coop.

I found a narrow, unsoiled stretch of mattress and lay down. My hand brushed a tightly folded piece of paper.

I unraveled it. It read, "Today is Wednesday, October 14th. On Monday the 19th, be in the cafeteria at 6:30 am. Freedom is coming. D and J. PS, eat this or flush it."

I couldn't believe it. Someone cared. There was some sort of resistance to this totalitarian nightmare.

Three days later, I felt that familiar quickening, the one I felt nearly a decade ago when my Pa put my first baby inside me. Daniel, a helmsman, got me pregnant. I felt it in my tummy. Science says it isn't possible, but it's real. Just like how my nipples leak milk when the baby's daddy is near. Not in any biology book, but real all the same.

3

THE CHICKEN COOP

They tested me, and sure as shit, I was pregnant with Daniel's baby. "A ripe orchard" was what the custodians called it. They moved me to the chicken coop on the 18th of October, just one day before the scheduled rendezvous in the cafeteria. I left the crusty blanket with pride. Spilling seed is a crime for seedsmen, but orchardmen can touch themselves all they want. Doctors say it helps the seed take root. It's encouraged. So they can just wash that filthy blanket and give it to the next orchardman.

The chicken coop looks like a men's prison in a foreign country where all the inmates are the same race. Monachee look a lot alike. We have black hair with loose curls. There's a bump on the back of our skull, the "fuck handle" as the crudest of the helmsmen like to call it. And then, of course, there's our huge anatomy between our legs. It varies a lot, but the smallest is bigger than any helmsman's.

In the chicken coop, we sleep on bunk beds stacked three high. The aisles between the beds are only two feet wide, so most of us have to crab-walk sideways, or our shoulders get bruised.

"Shepard!" It was Ben Scholls, a neighbor from Goochland. We went to school together before the population crisis ripped us from our homes. Now, on account of his anatomy, he's a seedsman.

"Ben, how ya been?"

"Fucking fantastic." His face betrayed the sarcasm. He looked to be six months pregnant. That's when you really start to feel it.

"Yeah, me too. Got a brand new bun in the oven." My smile wasn't any more sincere than his. We embraced. He smelled like home.

Ben said something but my mind was on whatever was happening the following morning. I wanted to see if Ben knew about it.

"Ben, what are your plans for breakfast tomorrow?"

Ben frowned. "Same plans I have every morning: wake up, wash up, and eat. Why? You got plans?"

I shook my head, watching Ben's eyes for a glimmer of shared knowledge, but it wasn't there. He wasn't part of the plan, whatever that was.

At 6:28 am on the 19th, I went to the cafeteria. A half dozen orchardmen from various dorms stood in a semicircle. There were no seedsmen. We scanned the room, trying to figure out if it was real or a trap. Jedediah walked in and smiled. He was the only seedsman in the bunch. He motioned us into the kitchen with his head. Silently, in twos and threes, we headed down a hallway leading to a loading dock.

Three armed custodians protected the door while they waited for the morning meat to arrive. One was tall and skinny, one was short and fat, and the other was a beefy older man with seniority. The senior custodian stepped forward.

"Jedediah, what are all these ripe orchards doing here?"

"Well, sir, they're trying out for kitchen duty. They're helping me and the others with the meat."

The senior custodian winked at Jed. "Sounds like a plan."

Jedediah nodded, but the short guy said, "That don't make a lick of sense. These orchards is stuffed. Ain't you stuffed too, Jed?"

Jed nodded.

"The doctor would kill us if we let any y'all work."

The senior custodian whirled around and spat. "Ain't no fuckin' doctors here."

The tubby little custodian was undeterred. "And where's the rest of Jed's crew?"

Jed shrugged. "With all this help, all but one of us gets to sleep in. I drew the short straw."

I later found out that Jed's crew were tied up in a utility closet and beat half to death, but I'm getting ahead of myself.

The red lights flashed, signaling a truck was pulling in. The custodians opened the loading dock door. I wasn't watching, but some kind of "accident" happened with the little custodian. The tall, skinny one smiled at us and dragged him off.

"Go on, get in!" The senior custodian shooed us into the back of the empty truck. We sat on some moving blankets. The truck driver handed off a wad of bills just before the senior custodian slammed the door shut, shrouding us in darkness. The truck started up and drove away.

"Free at last." We started singing the words to that old spiritual. "I thank God I'm free at last."

We couldn't have been more wrong.

4

WELCOME TO CASTLE ST. JOHN

The truck was on the road for a really long time. We had no water, no food, no toilet. Most Monachee are born with a sort of compass in their heads. We can tell which direction we're going. We agreed we were heading west, but a little bit north too. We got in the truck before the sunrise, and it was dark again outside. The air started to smell like a big city. We were creeping along in traffic. The truck exited the freeway, then came to a stop fifteen minutes later.

We were inside a compound with a great stone castle. As my eyes adjusted to the city lights, I recognized the skyline of Chicago in the distance. We were greeted by a host of armed custodians. They herded us into the castle. Daniel St. John smiled warmly at the top of a grand staircase.

"Gentlemen, welcome to Castle St. John. The custodians will show you to your rooms. Breakfast is at 7:00 am, followed by Orientation. Sleep well, all of you."

I shared a room with two orchardmen from the same hospital as me. The beds were more like cots, but they were better than the narrow rows of bunk beds in the chicken coop.

After introductions, we got to talking.

Guy, a Monachee from Tennessee, asked the obvious, "Why are we here?"

I shrugged, but Tyler, a Kentucky Monachee, had a theory. "He's keeping us safe for some reason. I think he has a way to get us to a free country where we can start over."

My mind went to a dark place. "I think he wants us to himself. He's hung big. He got me pregnant."

"Me too," said Guy.

"Me as well," said Tyler.

I continued my own theory. "He wants our babies and he knows the hospital would figure out what he's doing. They would never let him have a half-breed."

"Maybe he's gonna experiment on us." Guy's theory sounded true.

A custodian poked his head in and smiled. "Gentlemen, you'll need your rest. Go to sleep." He winked at me. I think it was some gay shit. And I liked it.

Breakfast was the first real home cooked food we'd had in years. There were eggs, waffles, bacon, sausage and ham. I had cream in my coffee for the first time since I'd been snatched. The room was filled with Monachee from all over Appalachia. You could tell by their looks. West Virginia Monachee look a lot alike, but they look completely different from Virginians. And the Carolina Monachee sometimes have auburn hair and freckles. There were a couple dozen of us. Apparently we weren't the first to arrive. The six of us from the truck were seated at our own table. I extended a friendly hand towards a Virginian Monachee man seated at the next table. He shook his head and swatted my hand away.

"You'll get us both killed," he whispered through his teeth.

Two custodians came running. The one who winked at me last night spoke. "What's going on here?"

The other man remained slouched, picking at his food.

"You, Shepard, what did he say?"

"He told me we wasn't allowed to talk."

"He's right."

The other custodian went to punch me, but my custodian stopped him.

"Don't rough 'em up. They're heavy with child."

Orientation was in a massive ballroom on the ground floor. The six of us rattled around like beebees in a boxcar. My custodian was in charge of this part.

"Gentlemen, welcome to the Castle. My name is Clyde but you can call me Clydsdale." He adjusted a massive lump on his right leg. "You are all guests of Daniel St. John. As such, you will need to obey the rules around here."

Clyde proceeded to rattle off a long list of do's and dont's that sounded like the rules in a Soviet prison..

"Breakfast is at 8:00 every morning, and you will arrive on time. You will do as you are told. You will not fraternize with members outside your truckload. You address me, my fellow custodians, and Daniel as "Sir.". If you ask questions any time after this orientation, you will be punished. Lunch is at noon and dinner is at five, but you will not always be able to attend if you're occupied. As you know Daniel has impregnated all of you. You will carry the babies to term. Anyone who terminates their pregnancy, either accidentally or purposely will be punished. You may not leave the compound. Anyone attempting escape will be terminated. Oh, and uh, there's chocolate ice cream for dessert tonight. Any questions? Ask them now because this is your one chance."

Guy raised his hand. "Why do we call you Clydesdale?"

Clyde grinned. "Well I ain't no heir to the Budweiser fortune. You'll find out soon." Clyde adjusted his monster package a second time. Guy was pretty dense.

"Is that it for questions?"

All our hands shot up.

He winked at me. "You, handsome."

"Why are we here?"

"I ain't permitted to answer that. I can tell you that you're in good hands, as long as you comply with our rules. If you don't, heaven help you."

Tyler asked, "What's Daniel trying to accomplish?"

"You orchardmen are so predictable. You're asking the same question a different way. You all do that. Every time."

Guy said, "But you haven't answered any of our questions!"

Clyde nodded. "True. Fair is fair. I'll answer one. They call me Clydesdale 'cuz I'm hung like a horse."

"No shit, Sherlock." One of the men who wasn't my roomie had made a mistake.

Clyde gestured to one of the custodians, who took out a Colt 45.

"You think just because you're pregnant you're immune? Daniel can replace you."

I watched as Clyde tried to silently telegraph to the other custodian. It told me something important. As long as we have a baby inside us, they can't hurt us. That was our only power.

The truck was on the road for a really long time. We had no water, no food, no toilet. Most Monachee are born with a sort of compass in their heads. We can tell which direction we're going. We agreed we were heading west but a little bit north, too. We got in the truck before the sunrise, and it was dark again outside. The air started to smell like a big city. We were creeping along in traffic. The truck exited the freeway. It came to a stop fifteen minutes later. The rear doors flew open.

Our eyes adjusted to the feeble light that blinded us after so many hours of total darkness.

We were inside a compound with a great stone castle. As my eyes adjusted to the city lights, I recognized the skyline of Chicago in the distance. We were greeted by a host of armed custodians. They herded us into the castle. Daniel St. John smiled warmly at the top of a grand staircase.

"Gentlemen, welcome to Castle St. John. The custodians will show you to your rooms. Breakfast is at 7:00 am, followed by Orientation. Sleep well, all of you."

I shared a room with two orchardmen from the same federal hospital as me. The beds were more like cots, but they were better than the narrow rows of bunk beds in the chicken coop.

After introductions, we got to talking.

One roommate was Guy, a Monachee from Tennessee. He asked the obvious, "Why are we here?"

I shrugged, but Tyler, a Kentucky Monachee, had a theory. "He's keeping us safe for some reason. I think he has a way to get us to a free country where we can start over."

My mind went to a dark place. "I think Daniel wants us to himself. He's hung big. He got me pregnant."

"Me too," said Guy.

Tyler's eyes widened. "Me, too.".

I continued my theory. "He wants our babies. He knows the hospital would figure out what he's doing. They would never let him have a half-breed. They always go to the experiment centers."

"Maybe he's gonna experiment on us or our babies." Guy's theory sounded true.

A big, strapping hunk of a custodian poked his blond head through the and smiled warmly. "Gentlemen, you'll need your rest. Go to sleep." He winked at me. I think it was some gay shit. And I liked it.

BREAKFAST WAS THE FIRST REAL HOME-COOKED FOOD we'd had in years. There were eggs, waffles, bacon, sausage and ham. I had cream in my coffee for the first time since I'd been snatched. The room was filled with Monachee from all over Appalachia. You could tell by their looks. West Virginia Monachee look a lot alike, but they look different from Virginians. And the Carolina Monachee sometimes have auburn hair and freckles. There were a couple dozen of us. Apparently, we weren't the first to arrive. The six of us from the truck were seated at our own table. I extended a friendly hand towards a fellow Virginian Monachee man sitting at the next table. He shook his head and swatted my hand away.

"You'll get us both killed," he whispered through his teeth.

Two custodians came running. The one who'd winked at me last night spoke. "What's going on here?"

The other man remained slouched, picking at his food.

"You, Shepard, what did he say?"

"He told me we wasn't allowed to talk."

"He's right."

The other custodian went to punch me, but my custodian stopped him.

"Don't rough 'em up. They're heavy with child."

ORIENTATION WAS IN A MASSIVE BALLROOM ON THE ground floor. The six of us rattled around like beebees in a boxcar. My custodian was in charge of this part.

"Gentlemen, welcome to the Castle. My name is Clyde, but you can call me Clydesdale." He adjusted a massive lump on his right leg, chuckling at his own joke.

I was astonished to see a bulge like that on a normal man. "You are all guests of Daniel St. John. As such, you will need to obey the rules around here."

Clyde proceeded to rattle off a long list of do's and don'ts that sounded like the rules in a Soviet prison.

"Breakfast is at 8:00 every morning, and you will arrive on time. You will do as you are told. You will not fraternize with members outside your truckload of six. You address me, my fellow custodians, and Daniel as "Sir.". If you ask questions of us any time after this orientation, you will be punished. Lunch is at noon, and dinner is at five, but you will not always be able to attend if you're occupied."

When I heard that word, 'occupied,' I felt a cold chill. What would we be doing besides lying around gestating? Was this a chain gang or a hospital?

Clyde continued. "As you probably know. Daniel has impregnated all of you. You will carry the babies to term. Anyone who terminates their pregnancy, either accidentally or purposely, will be punished. You may not leave the compound. Anyone attempting escape will be put in isolation. Oh, and uh, there's chocolate ice cream for dessert tonight. Any questions? Ask them now because this is your one chance."

Guy raised his hand. "Why do we call you Clydesdale?"

Clyde grinned. "Well, I ain't no heir to the Budweiser fortune. You'll find out soon enough." Clyde adjusted his monster package a second time. Guy was pretty dense, and his puzzled look was almost laughable.

"Is that it for questions?"

All our hands shot up.

He winked at me. "You, handsome."

"Why are we here?"

"I ain't permitted to answer that. I can tell you that

you're in good hands as long as you comply with our rules. If you don't, heaven help you."

Tyler asked, "What's Daniel trying to accomplish?"

"You orchardmen are so predictable. You ask the same question in a different way. You all do that, every time."

Guy said, "But you haven't answered any of our questions!"

Clyde nodded. "True. Fair is fair. I'll answer one. They call me Clydesdale 'cuz I'm hung like a horse."

"No shit, Sherlock." It came from one of the men who wasn't a roommate. He'd made a mistake saying that.

Clyde gestured to one of the custodians, who took out a Colt 45.

"You think just because you're pregnant, you're immune? Daniel can replace you."

I watched as Clyde tried to silently telegraph to the other custodian with an almost imperceptible shake of his head. It told me something important. As long as we had a baby inside us, they couldn't hurt us. We were irreplaceable. That was our only power.

5

IN THE LABORATORY

After Orientation, we went to a makeshift hospital laboratory in the basement. Daniel wore a long white coat and rubber gloves.

"Gentlemen, welcome. You'll be given a battery of tests. I won't lie to you; it's going to be unpleasant at times, even painful. But most of it is no different from a regular prenatal checkup."

He started by taking our blood. A lot of it.

We were each ordered into a private room, where we were made to sit on a modified gynecologist's examination table that raised our backsides to eye level. Our feet rested in stirrups. After waiting an eternity, Daniel appeared and took swabs from the inside of my ass. That didn't hurt. Then he whipped out the speculum, inserting it cautiously in my butt. He talked to me as he spread me open.

"I'm measuring how far you can dilate. The average baby's head at birth is 13 inches in circumference. My penis is a mere eight inches around. Yours looks to be nearly 12 inches in circumference. We'll measure it soon. That is why Monachee are so perfectly suited for anal birth. Your unique anatomy lets you accept a member nearly as big as a baby. Like your father's was, god rest his soul."

"You knew my Daddy?'

Daniel smacked me hard. "Sorry, but you must remember the rules of orientation. No questions."

He applied a cloudy solution to the exposed parts of my anus.

"This is a tincture of cocaine. It will numb you down there for a few minutes. You may experience a mild euphoria."

He was right. I felt a sudden surge of pleasure out of proportion to anything that was happening. I felt like I was back on my family's farm, and Daddy was putting another baby in me. The feeling wore off. The doctor had a long metal hose inside me. I think he was looking at the baby.

"This is much safer than X-rays. In Germany, I hear they have found a way to observe the child with sound waves. For now, a scope will have to suffice. You are only six days pregnant, but Monachee's fetal development is accelerated. I can see the newborn growing in your colo-uteral pocket."

I didn't know what the hell he was saying. All I knew was the cocaine had stopped working, and I felt like I had a coffee can up my ass. I gritted my teeth.

"You're hurting me."

"Oh! Sorry. Here." He applied more cocaine, and I was on a cloud playing a harp with God.

When I came down, he was rotating the crank on the speculum to close me back up. When he removed it, I didn't fully retract. He wiped his hand with some sort of cream and put his hand inside me.

"That's nothing to do with the exam. I just like the sensation."

I was pretty loose because he easily slid in and out of me. My cock responded to Daniel's fist. In a matter of moments, my prick was pointed skywards and growing with each heartbeat. It throbbed. Daniel hit a spot that caused me to leak sticky clear cum. Daniel caught it on his tongue.

"Monachee pre-ejaculate is the finest. It's like Russian caviar. And coming from such a perfect specimen of manhood, it's intoxicating." He licked the head like an ice cream cone.

I get really turned on when a man compliments my size. I don't know why. All I know is that Daniel said all the right things while he tongued the tip.

In between slurps, he said, "Shepard, Shepard, your cock is the most beautiful monolith I have ever seen." Then, "I want you inside me."

"That's dangerous, sir."

He put a finger to my lips. "I live dangerously."

He lowered the table. He removed his doctor's coat to reveal that he was completely naked from the waist down. I saw his manhood swinging. Daniel coated my erection and his hole with surgical jelly. He put cocaine up inside, too. Facing me, he squatted down, crying out in pain.

"Ohhh!" It was a cry of pain mixed with intense pleasure. "You're huge."

I grew even bigger upon hearing the compliment.

"Ahh! Shit! Oh, Jesus! It's not fair!" Daniel kept pressing until my head slipped past the entrance. Daniel pounded the wall. "I can do this!"

I enjoyed watching him struggle. It was fuel for my erection. Inch by inch, his ass swallowed more of me. I had taken many men inside, but this was my first time entering a man. I'd never realized how different it would feel. It was nothing like touching myself. Daniel lifted his left side to help me move past the first part and deeper within. He lost his balance, sliding down hard and landing in my lap. Daniel stared at me, tears of pain in his eyes. His mouth gasped like a fish as he held his breath.

I said, "Breathe, sir."

He released his breath, shuddering.

Daniel said, "I hope it didn't do permanent damage." He chuckled. "You are so big. Too big."

He tried to stand and fell back in my lap. Instinct kicked in. I put my hands on his butt and lifted him, dropped him, lifted, dropped, until he got his sea legs. He humped my cock with passion.

I'd stroked off plenty of times. Whenever a guy is inside me, I usually get off. None of it is like what happened next.

My balls started moving like two cats fighting in a canvas sack. I tapped a reserve of sperm I never knew I had.

"Oh shit," I said, "I'm gonna come. It's dangerous."

"I don't care." Daniel poured powdered cocaine on the back of his hand and sniffed. "I'm invincible."

My balls churned. I swelled bigger than I ever had. Daniel sat in my lap, impaled on my pole. He stroked his big hard dick.

"I'm coming!" I let out a huge breath as I reached orgasm. In spurts, then a rushing river, I came inside Daniel.

"It's warm, Shepard. I can feel the warmth up inside me. So deep." With that, he threw his head back and came.

After a minute of catching our breath, Daniel stood up, letting my spent cock flop out of him. It landed on the table and dangled over the edge.

Daniel called for the doctor, who rushed in and grabbed a large test tube, holding it to the crevice between the cheeks.

"I can't hold it." Daniel deposited my sperm into the container. "There. Got my sample. Sorry if my methods were a bit unorthodox."

6

RISK OF ELECTRIC SHOCK

We six met frequently to discuss theories about Daniel's grand purpose. Tyler, Guy, and I searched out the other three from our truckload: Logan, Erasmus, and Stewart. Six heads were better than three.

The other three confirmed they were all in early-stage pregnancy from Daniel. It had to be a research center. Our minds wandered through the horrible possibilities. Transplanting a fertilized fetus to a helmsman's wife was one awful hypothesis. It seemed implausible. If that were possible, they'd already be doing it.

Erasmus went to college, so he had better ideas.

"Look, this guy gets off on fathering boys in the midst of a population crisis. He's probably some narcissist who wants the world to become overrun with his genes."

"In English," said Guy.

"What's growing inside us is half helmsman, half Monachee. Can it get girls pregnant? Could it be a girl?"

I shrugged, "All I know is it doesn't belong to us, and it's probably illegal."

Clyde, the custodian, walked by, adjusting his crotch. He made eye contact with me, tilted his head, and kept walking in that direction. I looked around the circle of men but none of them caught what was happening with the custodian.

"Hey, I gotta take a leak. I'll be right back." I ducked out of the room and down the hallway. When I turned the corner, I saw Clyde walking slowly. He opened a door and stepped in. The door was labeled, 'Danger. Risk of Electric Shock."

Whatever power equipment had been in the room was long gone. I surveyed the small space. It was tricked out like a sex dungeon. I heard the door lock behind me.

I spun and saw the custodian.

"Boy, kneel down!" Clyde bellowed commands. "Crawl to your master!"

I knew my part. "Yes, sir." I crawled across the cold concrete floor until I reached his feet.

"Lick my boots. Don't miss a spot, or you'll get the whip."

How did I get myself into this? More importantly, why did I like it? As I licked his black boots, I looked up at Clyde's cruel and handsome face. The thick bulge was throbbing in his polyester pants.

"Reach up and feel your master's cock."

I did. It wasn't more than seven inches long, but it was thicker than Daniel's.

"You like that cock, boy?"

I nodded. Clyde gently kicked my chin. "Say it!"

"Master, Sir, I love your big cock."

"Correct. Again." He smacked a riding crop against his palm.

"Master, Sir, I love your big cock."

"What are you gonna do with it, boy?"

I paused. I didn't know the right answer. I looked at him, bewildered.

"Are you gonna suck it?"

"Yes, Master, Sir, I'm gonna suck that huge cock."

"What else are you gonna do with it?"

"I'm gonna put it in me, Master Sir." I broke character. "Isn't that bad for the baby?"

I felt the riding crop on my rump. It stung.

"No questions! But I ain't long enough to do any damage, boy. I'm gonna stretch you out. Keep it up every day, and you'll thank me in nine months."

I was worried—not just about the baby, but about my life and even Clyde's.

As if in answer to my fears, I saw Daniel St. John step out of the shadows.

"It's alright, Shepard. You were hand-picked for this experiment. Clyde is proportioned just right—extremely thick but not very long. You'll see. Now undress for me."

I felt a sexual response at the sound of Daniel's voice. I removed my dungarees and blue denim shirt. They still don't make underwear for Monachee. I'm not really sure how they could. So, apart from my slippers, I was naked.

Daniel and Clyde both drew in a sharp breath.

Clyde's eyes were saucers. "Holy shit, that is the biggest orchardman I've seen. And I've seen a bunch."

Daniel had never seen my soft cock hanging just below the knee. He had played with it hard when he got me pregnant, but seeing it at rest was something else.

They directed me to a hanging leather chair called a sling. I lay back, my member dangling over the front.

Daniel tilted his head. Clyde took off his uniform. When he shucked his boxer shorts, I gasped.

"Looks pretty thick, don't it?" Clyde smiled proudly.

"Yes, Master, Sir. Very thick." Indeed, it was, and it was only half hard. Being only seven inches long, Clyde's cock appeared almost comical the more it grew. It only grew in girth. I could see he was no threat to the baby growing inside me. And he kept growing far past the point I would have wanted. It went from a beer can to a tomato can. Then, it surpassed my girth and entered territory no food could describe. It was like a newborn baby.

Daniel smiled, "Clyde is uniquely gifted for this training."

Clyde dipped his hand in Crisco and began fingering me. Daniel stroked himself gently.

Clyde said, "Don't worry. I go slow. It may take an hour, but we'll get this in you. We start with the hands and then step up to my cock." His voice was tender now, and I felt so relieved to hear that he was looking out for me.

"Thank you, Master, Sir."

Clyde said, "Call me 'Clyde' or 'Daddy'. It's okay, son. Out there, I'm 'Sir.' In here, I'm yours."

I held back my tears. That was the nicest thing anyone had said to me in six years.

While Clyde worked his hand into my hole, Daniel circled us so his beautiful, long cock stood at attention above my head.

"Lean back, Shep."

I let my head loll. The world appeared upside down.

Daniel squeezed my cheeks, forcing open my mouth. In one swift thrust, he mashed past my tonsils and down my gullet. He held it there until I gagged and flailed, and then he removed it. He repeated this choking pattern five or six times until, at last, I let him plow his full length down my throat. He tugged and shoved until I felt the slick precum coat my throat. Daniel humped in and out with great ease. I tasted his salty dribbles; it made my cock go from flaccid to fully erect in seconds, and it caught Clyde by surprise. He took a sharp blow to the chin. We all laughed.

The sight of my giant cock put Daniel over the edge. He covered my face with his warm, fertile essence.

⊛

AFTER WHAT SEEMED LIKE HOURS, CLYDE HAD managed to get his two closed fists into my hole.

"Ready, son?"

Clyde didn't wait for an answer. He pressed his head to my hole and pushed. It was worse than childbirth, if only because it was going in, not coming out. Clyde was thicker than my Pa. I had never been stretched so wide. When Clyde pulled back too far and his cock slipped out of me, I could feel a cold draft. He quickly put it back in me, pushing that cold air up into my bowels. I had felt this stretched once, giving birth to a huge boy who came from my Pa, who once was a hulking, muscled Monachee. I had been spoiled with so many of the seedsmen's slender cocks. Clyde wasn't Monachee, but his girth rivaled mine.

The pain was excruciating. Two fists seemed nothing compared to Clyde's bulky meat. I doubted I would ever feel pleasure with Clyde. He was just too big around. I could have fit a cereal bowl in there with better luck and less pain.

Then nature shone her mercy on me. Monachee men have powerful natural painkillers that are released only during birth. Apparently, my body decided, on its own, to release those hormones. In a split second, my body went from agony to intoxicating euphoria.

"Oh, Daddy. Do it harder, Daddy!" I wrapped my legs around Clyde's hips and pulled him closer to me.

"You like that, boy? You like that, don't you?"

"Yes! Yes! Harder!"

Clyde couldn't hide his huge grin. He obliged, smacking so hard into my butt that it clapped. His smile was not cruel; it was genuine happiness.

As if he could read my thoughts, he said, "This has never happened for me. You're the first dude who enjoys it."

I held his head close to mine. Our lips locked while

our tongues explored each other's mouths. It made me wet down there. I was in bliss.

Daniel cleared his throat. "No affection, Clyde. You know the rules."

Clyde regretfully pulled his mouth from mine and returned to lovemaking. He was good at reading thoughts, as was I. Unsupervised, we would have kissed our lips raw. In that instant, we both knew that we had fallen in love.

Suddenly, the prospect of a daily training session with Clyde seemed like Brer Rabbit's briar patch: a place meant for punishment with the opposite effect.

Clyde stroked my towering pole as he invaded my being. By now, I was awash in endorphins. A buzzer sounded as a red light came on.

"Excuse me." Daniel put it back in his pants and left the room.

Clyde returned to kissing me, which put me close to the edge. Apparently, it did the same for him.

"Oh fuck, Shepard, I'm gonna come."

"Me too."

Our breath synced up. My face screwed up in a grimace. I felt Clyde swell even bigger inside me. I had arrived. So had he. It was a beautiful moment. I felt my own warm fluids mingle on my face with Daniel's.

We came. Clyde stroked my hair, then put his tongue in my mouth. We kissed like lovers for five minutes until Clyde's manhood softened. He pulled out.

Clyde helped me out of the hanging leather chair. "Same time tomorrow."

It wasn't a question but a command. "Yes, Sir."

He mussed my hair playfully. "Clean up, boy. You're soaked."

Along the same hallway were the group showers. I limped into the changing room and shucked my clothes. I heard a wolf whistle. It was Guy.

"Damn, dude! We're all huge, but you are in another league."

I blushed. Guy leaned in and whispered. "I'd like to try and take that." He sniffed. "Whose cum is that? You look like you swam in glue."

I put my fingers to my lips. Spilled semen had been a deadly offense for custodians and seedsmen since the plague. I knew Clyde was likely exempt, given his special gift, but I didn't want any harm to come to him. Just thinking about him made my heart leap in my throat.

I rushed to the showers and cleaned the copious emissions from my ears, eyes, neck, and abdomen. As I washed, a small crowd of orchardmen joined me. As orchardmen, we varied in length and girth but were all far above average, too big for lovemaking, hence our roles as passive carriers. Nonetheless, I was the cock of the walk, hanging much lower and thicker than anyone else. As orchardmen, we were allowed to masturbate. So, it was no surprise when the shower room gradually dissolved into a circle jerk. Everyone looked at me, but no one dared talk or touch.

As the soap suds gathered at the root of my cock and washed over my balls, I felt stirrings in my recently spent loins. To be the object of attraction is an aphrodisiac for me. The circle jerk in my honor was a huge turn-on. And then something 'huge' 'turned on.' I stroked my pole until they invited me into the circle, passing me around so that everyone would get a chance to stroke, touch, tickle my extraordinary dick.

The crowd swelled. Soon the showers were packed with orchardmen grasping for a chance to hold the biggest cock that any had ever seen. We had to remain silent to prevent talking to other groups. But Guy sidled up near me and held my manhood firmly with two hands. He allowed a half dozen men to grasp hold, and in unison, they stroked swiftly up and down. The smell of male lust causes more lust to form. In this huge crowd, I was swimming in male sex hormones. We all were. I closed my eyes and pictured Clyde battering me with masterful, hard strokes.

It wasn't long before it began to rain in the shower room. Water washed away the rain, but more kept coming until we were glazed in the stuff. It smelled good, like buttered popcorn. I spent the next twenty minutes soaping and rinsing off parts of my body I had forgotten existed. Every nook and cranny was soiled with orchardmen's gyzm. I was the last to leave. Nobody even offered to help clean me up, not even Guy.

Normally, this empty sexual experience would leave me depressed or hopeless. But now that I had Clyde, I was unphased by the whole incident. I didn't even care that they had left me alone. I slept like a baby that night

7

THE EXERCISE

The next morning, I awoke with a nagging feeling in the back of my mind. I went to breakfast and sat with Guy. The fact that I chose Guy triggered the memory of what was eating at me. Why were we only allowed to speak with our truckload of orchardmen? Why was it okay for me to talk to Clyde, the custodian? What didn't Daniel want us all to know or figure out?

"Hello?" Guy woke me from my musings.

"Sorry, I was just thinking about things."

Guy laughed. "Reminiscing about the glazing you got?"

I shook my head. "I'm worried something's not right. Why does he want us compartmentalized? What doesn't he want us to know?"

A nearby stranger held his hand parallel to the table and lowered it in a gesture of silence. He couldn't talk to me, but he wanted me to know my questions were dangerous. I tried to ask indirectly. I said softly to Guy, "Do we go back to the coop once we give birth?"

The stranger looked around. He put his hand on his belly and held it out several inches from his navel—the gesture for a big belly.

I whispered to Guy, "We get impregnated again."

The stranger scratched his nose while slowly nodding.

A custodian was strolling down our aisle. I waited until he had passed. In a whisper, I said, "And if we refuse?"

The stranger held an index finger to his throat and made the throat-slash sign.

I had so many more questions, but that silenced me for now.

Clyde surprised me when he tapped his billy club on the table. "Shep, boiler room duty begins promptly at 10 a.m. Don't be late."

Guy laughed. "What's that all about?"

I shrugged.

At ten, I went to the room with the electric danger warning sign. Daniel and Clyde were waiting for me. Clyde's eyes sparkled when he looked at me. They helped me up into the leather chair, where I awaited another double stuffing.

Daniel went down my throat while Clyde worked his Crisco-covered hands into my rectum. The first finger went in easily, then two, three fingers – each finger more difficult and painful to take.

I concentrated on Daniel's presence in my throat. It slipped past the tonsils and into my throat. I gagged, but nothing came up. When I felt my face turn blue, I pulled back and breathed two sharp breaths before swallowing Daniel again. He thrust his hips, using my throat to stroke himself.

Clyde was making progress. He still had to get his other thumb in there. He stretched, played, swatted, and spanked until my hole relented and swallowed the second hand. He withdrew one then as he plunged it back in, he pulled the other out. He continued in a see-saw fashion until he could easily put two hands in and pull them out without effort.

I kept my attention on Daniel, who used me. It felt

like he didn't really care if I suffocated. He squeezed my throat to increase sensation. I couldn't breathe anyway. I lifted my head to get some air. He didn't wait for me to take a second breath. He thrust with abandon. I couldn't take it. Some of my breakfast came up and spilled out my nose and the corners of my mouth. Daniel ignored it. In fact, he picked up the pace. He threw me a rag to clean myself. The burning sting and vile stench in my nose made me want to puke again. I didn't try to fight it. The minute I was sent to the coop, I lost sovereignty over my body. I was resigned to forced sex peppered with the occasional pleasant encounter. I had to admit this was unpleasant, but I was still engorged with lust.

In one swift movement, Clyde shoved his absurd thickness inside. It didn't hurt. It helped that I found Clyde extremely attractive. I wrapped my hands around his butt and pressed him in all the way to the end. It was like childbirth, only better. I pushed him over and over, loving the sensation of my entire hole full of Clyde's cock.

Daniel was close. I felt my throat slicked with pre-cum. I took another breath and tasted the salty-sweet juice. I got in two breaths before Daniel plugged me up. His frenzied gyrations ended with my throat full of his sanctified essence. He pulled out and made sure the rest covered my face and neck. He held his softening penis at the base and smacked my face hard. He struck me with it a few more times before he pulled up his pants.

"Alright, gentlemen. Are we good here?"

"Yes, Boss," said Clyde.

"Yes, Sir."

Daniel smiled. "Alright, I will leave you two to continue the exercise."

Exercise. I wasn't sure what it meant. I took a risk and asked, "Clyde, what sort of exercise is this?"

Clyde was on another plane. His eyes were fluttering from the joy of plowing my ass.

"We're making sure you don't crush the baby. Now shut up and take this dick, boy."

"Yes, Master." That turned Clyde on even more. He pressed hard until his hips were touching my butt cheeks. He pressed against the junction, but he wasn't long enough to push through to the place where we conceive. That is exactly why Daniel chose him for this "exercise."

Despite my lack of choice in the matter, I wanted his enormity inside me. I wanted him to leave his infertile seed in me. I wanted him to use his tongue. Hell, he could stick his head up there for all I cared.

After several minutes, Clyde started snorting like a stallion. I reached up and felt for his nipple under his uniform. What I found was pure muscle with a nipple at the bottom of a massive pectoral muscle. When I found the nipple, Clyde threw his head back and climaxed. He stayed inside me until his log of bologna wilted into a beer can. My muscles would normally push him out, but I was so stretched I had no thrust. He just fell out. If only a baby could pass so easily!

Without me asking, Clyde kneeled, then tongued my ass. I could feel the hot breath from his nostrils. He licked in places no tongue had ever been. For a brief second, I thought he might really put his whole head up there!

"Shepard, I've been with a lot of orchardmen here at the Castle. None of them can hold a candle to your good looks. You're beautiful."

"Is that why I see your eyes sparkle when I walk in the room?"

Clyde blushed. Something he said stuck in my craw.

"You've been with a lot of guys here. Have you been with Tyler? Erasmus?" I couldn't believe I sounded like a jealous hen.

"Uh, those guys are in your truckload, right?"

I nodded.

"Nope. Only one per truckload. You're the pick of the litter."

I frowned. "But--?"

"Sorry, Shep. I would lose my job or worse if I kept answering these questions. I've already said way too much."

"Would they kill you?"

Clyde shrugged. "I hope not."

Something about the way he said it told me he was no stranger to violence. He is a custodian, after all. They see a lot. I had plenty of time to ask him questions. Seven or eight months. I hoped he would make love to me when my abdomen was so swollen, the navel would have turned inside out.

❧ 8 ❦

BEDPAN MIRE

On my way to the shower, I ran into Tyler, Guy, and Logan.

Tyler whistled. "Man, who glazed your donut?"

I shrugged. "A Monachee never tells."

The mood wasn't jovial. Logan said, "Have you seen Erasmus or Stewart?"

I shook my head.

Guy said, "None of us have. Where are they?"

I was slippery with cum and wanted to get to the showers as soon as possible. "Walk with me. You guys smell like you could use a shower."

As we walked, we spoke in hushed tones. Logan said, "Maybe they're on a different wing. It's a big castle."

Guy said, "Yeah, but they were on our wing when we got here. Why would they move them?"

I was worried. "Did you all get tested by Daniel?"

They all nodded. I wondered if they had their sperm sample taken the same way as me.

"Did he make you fuck him?"

Tyler said, "Don't be ridiculous. We went to the toilet and jacked off in a cup.'

As we dug deeper, the mystery only grew. Guy and I

were the only two who saw the stranger make the cut-throat sign.

"Guy, did you tell them what we heard from that lonely guy?"

Guy shook his head and held an index finger to his lips.

Logan said, "What? What did you hear?"

Guy had been a car salesman before the plague struck. He was a quick thinker. "We heard that if you talk back to a custodian, they suspend your shower and toilet privileges for a whole month. You get a bedpan and a sponge—that's it. The sponge doubles as toilet paper."

Tyler wrinkled his nose. "That's disgusting! Barbaric!"

We shushed Tyler.

The showers were empty, so I was able to clean myself up in time for lunch without any additional circle jerks.

The days turned into weeks. Every day, from 10:00 to noon, I sucked off Daniel and let Clyde have his way with me. I was a bird in a gilded cage. Clyde made captivity feel warm and reassuring. Our kisses grew ever more passionate. Just seeing Clyde made my sphincter relax. He didn't need to use his hands with me anymore. He entered me with very little resistance. One time, he made love to me for the full two hours, climaxing three times. When Daniel was in the room, we were less passionate. But the minute he left, we kissed and fucked like two high school kids.

Mata Hari was a German spy during World War I. She gathered intelligence by seducing British and French Officers. She was executed by firing squad after the war; nonetheless, her methods inspired me.

Neither Clyde nor I had used the L word. It was a work environment, not a motel bed. But I always got in a little pillow talk with him at the end of our sessions.

So far, I'd learned that he was never married (he identified as a gay top). He lived in the building. His shift was twelve hours, but those extra two hours with me meant that he was busy from ten until midnight. There wasn't another wing, but I dared not ask where our missing friends were. I was afraid of the answer.

In the third month, Logan disappeared. It was just Tyler, Guy, and me now. They begged me to ask my secret lover where he had gone, but a part of me knew the answer already. A helmsman's baby borne by a Monachee hadn't happened in recent history. Back in the pre-revolutionary days, there was a British Duke who was rumored to have impregnated a Monachee man from Hendrix Hill. The Monachee man carried the baby to term. So there's British royal blood in the Monachee clan, specifically my clan from Virginia. There are hundreds of stories of regular folks who have somehow gotten one of us pregnant; they always end in miscarriage or stillbirth. I feared that Erasmus, Logan, and Stewart had miscarried. The finger across the neck was as far as I wanted to go in my thoughts.

I know Tyler and Guy knew this, too. We had long stopped talking about it.

In my fifth month at the Castle, Guy pulled me aside, his eyes wide with fear. "Shep, I lost a lot of blood this morning. I think I..." He collapsed in tears. That was a bad sign; miscarriages release a bunch of fucked up hormones that make men emotional and weepy.

I held Guy in my arms, letting him release those tears. I wanted him to face his imminent death with some degree of dignity. The next morning, he wasn't at breakfast; I never saw him again.

9

WASP'S NESTS

Tyler was showing. He'd been with Daniel a few weeks before I had. We sat at breakfast, picking at our food.

Tyler had taken some business classes in community college. It may as well have been a foreign language when he asked me, "What's his revenue model?"

"What?"

Tyler stabbed three blueberries with his fork. "How does Daniel make money?"

I shrugged. "He probably didn't earn it. He got it from Dad."

Tyler shook his head. "No, he's a self-made man. You can tell. This place is a business. I just don't know what he's selling."

I had sucked his cock a hundred times, but I never thought to ask him a question. It's hard to ask a question when your airway is blocked. 'I'm gonna find out.'

After breakfast, I reported to my session. My throat had grown used to Daniel so he went in easy. My gag reflex was on hiatus. Daniel was fond of rubbing my tummy and kissing it while he used my throat for his pleasure. It had become a ritual that brought me joy despite the power dynamics.

Daniel closed his eyes and moaned. "Ohhh Shep,

you are the best cocksucker ever." I appreciated the compliment, even if it was coming from my captor. Meanwhile, in my nether regions, I could feel Clyde's wide presence, stretching me, bringing me to the edge of ecstasy.

Daniel never took very long. In a few short minutes, he pulled out and used his hands to release all over my face.

I decided to risk a question to see what would happen. "Daniel, do you get off this easily with the others?"

He smiled. "Knowing that you're carrying my child turns me on. I'm pretty quick with all my orchardmen, but you're the sexiest. Look at that marvel! It's like an elephant trunk."

As if he were Daniel's partner at a fairgrounds cookware demonstration, Clyde held it aloft and kissed the head. He got a few swirls of his tongue in, which made me hard. Getting hard with Clyde was proof that I enjoyed it too much to call it anything but lovemaking.

I decided to dare another question while Daniel wiped off and put his pants back on.

"What's your revenue model?"

It was too direct. Daniel slapped my face hard. My cheek stung. Daniel handed me a towelette to wipe off, ignoring my hurt look. I glimpsed Clyde, who wasn't angry at me like I thought he would be. He glowered in Daniel's direction but didn't let him see the scowl.

"Alright, kids, have fun." Daniel left us alone.

The altercation had left Clyde limp. He pulled out.

"What was that?"

I shrugged. "I don't understand how he makes money, is all."

Clyde was in conflict. He was angry at his boss, but telling me anything could mean death.

"You know what? Fuck it. Fuck Daniel. Here's what's up. Daniel gets off on getting orchardmen pregnant. If a baby carries to term, he sells it on the black market. There are rich bitches out there willing to pay two million to have a half-Monachee child. They're fertile, and they can be boys or girls. Now I've said too much."

"I won't breathe a word of it." I lied.

Clyde looked at me sweetly as he wiped away the blood from my nose. "Shep, do you love me?"

"Yes. Do you love me?"

He nodded. We kissed until his member reached its thickness. The sex felt so much better after we had confessed our love. Going in, he loved me. Pulling back, he loved me. And since he was going at a rapid pace, he loved me a thousand times. A warm sensation began deep in my gut and spread. It vibrated. I was vibrating. This was a first.

"I'm quivering."

Clyde nodded. "I can feel it. Oh, that's strong."

"What is it?" I was afraid it was the baby.

Clyde's eyes fluttered. "Oh god, keep doing that, babe."

I didn't have much choice. "Am I losing the baby?"

Clyde shook his head. "You, my love, are having an anal orgasm."

He was right. I loved him terribly. It made me quiver, then shake, moan, and scream. I had never been fucked like this. Clyde was the perfect fit in every way. That big slab of meat started pushing harder and faster until Clyde's hips were a blur. I thrashed and bucked, but Clyde stayed inside me, making my insides come. My cock stood at 90 degrees straight up in the air. Precum started gushing down the foreskin in rivers. Clyde leaned forward and tasted it.

"Oh! Ohh! Baby, I'm gonna come. I'm gonna come."

At the exact moment I felt the familiar warm flow inside me, the orgasm intensified like a hive of wasps buzzing inside me. My cock shot straight up in the air, raining down over and over until we both were covered in it. The orgasm wouldn't stop, and the vibrations kept Clyde hard, so he made love to me again without stopping to smoke or drink a beer.

All told, that day, we climaxed five times together. We had missed lunch by the time we were through. Even after Clyde withdrew, the vibrations continued. I cramped from the sudden absence of his fat, reassuring member inside me. We had to stop kissing so my orgasm could die down. After twenty minutes of post-coital bliss, I finally stopped shaking.

I looked into Clyde's eyes. "You love me. You're going to help me. Together, we'll live a better life somewhere else."

Clyde nodded

10

I HEARD A RUMOR

At morning announcements, Daniel looked unwell. His face was grey, and he kept mopping up sweat. He handed the microphone off and excused himself. When I got to the boiler at 10:00 am, it was just me and Clyde. I asked what was up with Daniel.

Opening the Crisco, he said, "After sex."

I couldn't argue with that. I wanted him so bad. With ease, he slipped inside me. He wasn't fully hard. I loved the feeling as more and more blood filled his cock, so that it touched everywhere and then stretched even more. Not having to suck Daniel let me concentrate on Clyde, who appreciated all the extras I had to give. I played with his nipples until he was at maximum size inside me. His gentle thrusts grew more forceful until he set off another quivering orgasm. I thrashed and vibrated, kissing Clyde passionately.

"Damn, Shepard, you are so perfect!"

His words, coupled with the spasms in my body, brought my cock to attention. Clyde tried but couldn't get the head in his mouth. Instead, he licked it and used both hands to slide up and down the length. I leaned back, grateful to be able to breathe without Daniel blocking my airway. Clyde surprised me when he tweaked and twisted my nipples. The orgasm intensified. I imagined this is how women feel when they have a good man with a good dick inside them.

Clyde thrust in and out, sometimes pausing fully exposed to the open air before plunging all the way back in me. He flexed his hips, trying to lift my ass higher with his cock. It almost worked. It also made me leak. Clyde licked at it like a kid with a melting ice cream cone. Each time he flexed his hips, more precum came out. With the vibrations growing more and more intense, I lost the power of speech.

"Ngggghaaaaah" was the closest I could come to saying something. Clyde dutifully humped me until I couldn't hold back. I shot sperm skywards; it rained down on us in thick droplets. The vibrations continued.

Clyde was close. I clamped his teats between my thumb and forefinger, twisting and tugging at them.

"Oh shit, Shepard, you're gonna make me cum."

I didn't stop. I wanted his cum inside me. I leaned forward and gently bit down on one nipple, rubbing it with my tongue.

"Oh shit! Oh shit! Oh fuck!" Clyde had arrived. "I love you, man!" He kissed me hard while he erupted inside me, making my ass sticky and warm.

"I love you, too, Clyde."

He remained collapsed forward, his cheek to my belly, breathing in great gasps. He had fucked the wind right out of himself. He was still inside me, and I was still vibrating, so he swelled up again. He planted his lips on mine while our tongues explored each other's mouths. He could make me precum any time he wanted with just a lift of his hips. Biting and tonguing his teat was effective at bringing him to orgasm. Once I started vibrating, it was just a matter of minutes before he would come again. I alternated kissing him with biting his nipples. When we weren't kissing, he licked my pole clean of any precum he had squeezed out of me. The vibrations were stronger this time. Without warning, Clyde ejaculated. I was so surprised, it made me climax again. Clyde handed me a handkerchief and used another to wipe my cum from his hair and face.

Clyde climbed up into the chair. It was built for one, but we managed. He put a protective arm across my chest and played with my nipple.

"Clyde," I said, "what's wrong with Daniel?"

He removed his arm but didn't leave the chair. He crossed his arms across his massive chest. "You got to promise not to tell."

I nodded. "I swear it."

"It's just a rumor, but one of the custodians told me that he let a Monachee screw him, and he somehow got pregnant."

I wondered if that Monachee was me.

"But he doesn't have a uterine pocket! That's not possible. Only we can get pregnant."

This was the accepted medical truth. There's a Monachee superstition that regular men could get pregnant from Monachee, just like women. Rumors floated around about a Monachee who went to college and got his male roommate pregnant.

Clyde shrugged. "Like I said, it's a rumor."

We lay in silence, but my brain was racing. Was I the only Monachee who'd been inside him? The other guys from my truck said they came in a cup. I decided it had to be me. There had been no new truckloads, and he had told me I was the finest specimen. He couldn't have known I could get him pregnant. Or maybe he merely had the flu.

Clyde nudged me and pointed to his crotch. The monster was rising and swelling again. Seeing it caused a stirring in my loins.

"You want to go at it again?"

I smiled. "I thought you'd never ask."

As Clyde buttoned his shirt and buckled his belt, I asked probing questions.

"Does Daniel let Monachee men screw him often?"

Clyde frowned. "He doesn't do that at all. He's a total top, like me."

"Then how can he have gotten pregnant?"

Clyde shook his head. "Like I said, I heard one time he let one of you do it to him about five months ago. But it's hearsay."

That sealed it. Daniel was carrying my child, just as I was pregnant with his.

I hit the showers. Tyler was there. He came close to me. "What's wrong with Daniel?"

I felt bad when I shrugged. "Maybe the flu."

Tyler playfully slapped my dick. "How hard is it to carry that thing around? Does it hurt your back?"

I slapped back. "I know yours is only half the size, Tyler, but it's still useful."

We both laughed. In the back of my mind, crazy was starting to form. I wanted my baby. I wanted both of my babies. How could I possibly manage such madness? I needed to talk to Clyde.

"Shepard, are you okay?"

"What?"

Tyler said, "I asked you a question a bunch of times and you didn't answer. You went somewhere else."

"Sorry, Tyler. What was the question?"

"Nothing. I just wondered what it's like to have the biggest dick ever."

"You'd have to ask my dad."

Tyler laughed.

I headed to the bedroom for a nap. Once we started to show, our only jobs were to shower and gestate. We weren't allowed to cook, clean, make our beds, or even rinse a cup. It was all handled by servants. We just had to maintain proper hygiene and grow a baby.

The door to the bedroom was ajar, but a sign said, "Do Not Enter. Cleaning."

Inside, two servant women made the beds, scrubbed the floors, gathered dirty plates, and chatted. I hung outside the door and eavesdropped.

"I was the one who took him to the hospital," said a woman with a Chicago accent. It sounded like "haspital."

"My goodness. Is he really sick?" The second woman had more of a southern drawl

"Holy smokes. You're not gonna believe this. He's pregnant!"

The Southern lady said, "Land's sake, that simply isn't possible. Is it?"

"Oh ya. It's happened before. Monachee legend and all, but it sounded real to me."

"But that would mean he's homosexual."

The Chicago lady said, "Well, that's illegal now. They'll be throwing him in jail when he's well."

The Southern woman said, "I suppose we'll never know who the father is. He could be dead now."

"No. That's just the thing! He's here. In this room. Biggest schlong you ever seen. I'm surprised he didn't kill Daniel when he stuck it in."

I quietly moved away from the door and bolted down the hallway. A custodian chased me.

"Hey! You there! Don't run! You'll hurt the baby!"

"Sorry, sir!" I slowed down. I didn't know where to go.

I thought maybe the electrical room would be a good place to gather my thoughts. I opened the door and heard two men fucking.

"Shit! Ouch! Goddamn you!" It was Tyler.

"It's for the baby. Relax." My heart sank. That voice could only be Clyde.

I closed the door quietly, trembling with fear, rage, and sadness.

I returned to my room just as the cleaning ladies were leaving. The one from Chicago was short and squat. She whispered, "That's the one."

The other was a tall beauty. She looked me up and down. In her drawl, she said, "You're a handsome one, aren't you?"

"Excuse me." I brushed past them and slammed the door. I buried my head in my pillow and sobbed. Finding out I had sired a child that might kill Daniel was hard enough. Learning that others knew about it was too much. Seeing the man whom I loved fucking my best friend was hot Appalachian coal stuffed into my heart. I cried myself to sleep. There were no dreams. It was lunchtime, but I didn't wake until dawn.

❧ 12 ❧

CHICKEN RUN

Alone, early in the morning, I began to plot and scheme. I would give Clyde the benefit of the doubt. He'd had to fuck Tyler. He had a job, and that was to stretch us out to make for easier birth. I'm a lot more than a stretched rectum to him; we love each other.

As much as I hated Daniel, I had to accept that he was carrying my child, and I was carrying his. He was an unwelcome member of my family, but a member, nonetheless. Maybe it's some hormonal thing, but knowing someone has your baby softens you. I had to let go of my hate and focus on rescuing Daniel. They were going to terminate the pregnancy and throw him in jail. Then what would become of the castle?

At breakfast, Tyler winced when he sat down beside me.

"You started the sessions?"

Tyler nodded. "Clyde is a fucking monster."

I had never told Tyler about our mutual love, and I wasn't about to.

"Didn't like it?" I smiled, but inside was seething.

Tyler said. "Hated it. He made sure it was awful. Said some shit like, 'You aren't worthy of this.'"

Jealousy is a useless emotion. It causes wars, murder, and all kinds of evil in this world. I wasn't jealous of a guy who had no choice but to sleep with my lover. In truth, he was a victim of this barbaric castle prison. The boiling rage that accompanies jealousy is unavoidable, but I knew in my heart it was misguided. I decided to tell Tyler what I knew.

When I finished, Tyler sat in stunned silence. Then he said, "I'm sorry about your boyfriend. If I had known..."

I smiled. "Neither of you could do anything. It's his job. I'm sorry he was rough with you!"

"What are we going to do?"

It was a good question. "I'm still working on it."

⚜

AT 10:00 AM, I REPORTED TO THE ELECTRICAL ROOM. Clyde was there, stiff and ready for action. I really wanted to talk to him first, but I couldn't deny him his need for pleasure. I was cool at the start. The remnants of my jealousy were putting a pall over the act. But when he swelled to full girth and bucked his hips upward, I came to life. Soon, I was in love again, vibrating with internal orgasm.

"Shepard, you're so fucking beautiful!" He held my fuck handle, pulled my skull close to his, and kissed me with his tongue.

I was in ecstasy, but my urgent need to tell Clyde what was happening overshadowed any pleasure. I nursed on his nipples with bites so strong he cried aloud. "Jesus, Shep, that hurts."

I withdrew my teeth. Clyde said, "Don't stop. I didn't say to stop."

So, I gnawed like a teething baby. I was only semi-hard. With Clyde, I had always been at full attention.

He pressed harder, hoping to turn me on more, but it didn't work. He was perturbed, but it didn't stop him from reaching orgasm.

Afterward, I said, "I need to talk to you."

Clyde nodded. "I figured as much."

"Daniel is carrying my child."

Clyde blinked. "Shit. That's weird. Like really weird. How did it happen?"

"During my initial tests, he made me do it with him. That was me you heard about."

Clyde shook his head. "He knew about the royal bloodline, and he knew you were a descendant. He said so. That's why he picked you out from the truckload."

"So my other fellow passengers could die."

"Die?" Clyde raised an eyebrow.

"You know what happens to them when they miscarry."

"They're released. I often drive them downtown so they can catch a train."

I was astonished. "Then what?"

"Some of them get caught and thrown back in a federal hospital. But a lot of them make it to Canada or Mexico."

"I thought they were killed."

Clyde put a hand on my knee. "I'm so sorry the world is doing this to you."

I looked at him. He meant it. "What's in Canada or Mexico?"

"Human rights."

That had been the problem with my long-range planning, and now it was solved.

"Clyde, will you go to Canada with me?"

"We gotta get Daniel out of that hospital, Shep."

I sighed. "That wasn't what I asked."

Clyde realized his blunder. "Of course, I'll go to Canada with you, although Puerto Vallarta sounds a lot nicer."

"Yeah, but Mexico is 1,500 miles from here. Canada seems much closer. Would we be safe?"

Clyde nodded. "Mexico is more welcoming of Orchards. Canada might turn you away - they're facing an immigration crisis. Between here and Mexico, you wouldn't come across many patrol units; the danger is just plain folks. It's regular citizens who will recognize your kindness and turn you in. Daniel has a private jet at Midway Airport. We could fly to Mexico."

I said, "What if Daniel doesn't want to leave?"

"He's going to be arrested or executed. He has to leave."

I was worried. "What about all the other orchardmen? What will become of them?"

"Let me worry about it. First, I'm going to the hospital to get Daniel out."

"I'm coming with you."

"No, you're going to stay here and get people ready to run."

"The custodians..."

"I'll take two custodians with me and let the others know what's happening. I need you to gather the orchardmen in the dining hall and explain what's happening. The custodians are going to drive them to El Paso and smuggle them into Juarez."

With my marching orders, I went from bedroom to bedroom, announcing the gathering in the dining hall. An hour later, I stood at Daniel's podium, flanked by custodians.

"Gentlemen, thank you for coming. I have grave news."

The room fell to a hush.

"Daniel St. John is in the hospital. You may have heard rumors, but I'm here to give you a truthful update."

The men sat quietly. I realized that they were afraid to speak.

"First, the ban on conversation is lifted. We may all speak freely."

This caused a sudden outbreak of chatting. The custodians reflexively raised their clubs, then realized they had no need to stop it.

One orchardman called, "Who put you in charge?"

"It's a complicated matter, but I assure you I am just here to inform you. The custodians are still in charge."

As the hubbub died down, I continued. "Daniel, the father of all our babies, is now himself pregnant."

The room exploded. I heard cries of, "It ain't fuckin' possible!" and "This is a load of horse shit!"

I held my hands aloft to quiet the dozens of men.

"I learned a lot in the past 24 hours, and I want to share it with you. First of all, the men we all feared were dead were not killed; they were driven to Union Station and set free. We're going to do the same for every orchardman here, but we'll take you over the Mexican border, where you will be granted asylum."

One older Monachee said, "What if we don't want to go?"

I paused. "Staying here will ensure your captivity. You'll be returned to the nearest Federal Hospital. Daniel is likely going to be arrested, and this place will be no more."

The look of confusion on everyone's face was not what I'd hoped for.

"Listen, in the New United States, no helmsman is allowed to have homosexual sex for any purpose but procreation. Daniel's pregnancy is a capital offense. This whole operation is illegal. We are stolen property. He's at the hospital gravely ill. There's no future for any of us here."

We had no possessions, nothing to pack but our slippers and pajamas. I prayed every minute that Clyde would return. My mind kept harping on the fact that

Daniel was carrying my child, which made me worry for him too.

Daniel owned six passenger vans; each seated eight, but you could get away with ten. There were fifty-three of us, so we could all fit, except Clyde was out retrieving Daniel with the sixth van. That meant three of us would have to wait.

I leaped up on a table and cried out, "Three of us need to wait for the last van."

Tyler volunteered immediately. He knew it was dangerous, but he valued our friendship over all else. The older Monachee fellow who didn't want to go said he would stay with us.

The vans left in ten-minute intervals. At the end of the hour, we were the only three left, along with a couple of handsome custodians. We introduced ourselves.

"Brian," said the shorter of the two custodians. He had deep green eyes and a mustache that suited him well.

"Enrico," said the taller custodian. He was a light-skinned Mexican with freckles. He wore black cowboy boots with his uniform.

"Lonnie," the older man extended his hand. He was eight months pregnant, ready to pop.

If I weren't so worried, I might have found this a sexy bunch. Enrico had a face like Clark Gable. Brian's smoldering green eyes set my hormones ablaze. But this wasn't the time or place for group sex.

We all hovered in the security room, watching the cameras anxiously for any sign of the white van. Nothing.

Another hour ticked by; I went from worried to distraught. Then, in the distance, we heard sirens. In my heart, I knew they were coming for us.

Tyler said, "Crap, they're here." He pointed to the monitor, which showed a cavalcade of cop cars pulling up to the fortified gates of the castle compound. Brian, the shorter custodian, grabbed my arm. Enrico grabbed Lonnie and Tyler.

"Ow! Where are you taking us?" I was regretting my decision to lead this escape.

Brian winked a gorgeous green eye and said, "Don't worry. We're safe."

THE UNDERGROUND
RAILROAD

The two custodians led us down a long hallway that was off-limits to orchardmen. We descended a spiral staircase that seemed never to end. When at last we reached the bottom, there was a dimly lit dirt hallway that dead ended at a brick wall. Enrico tapped two bricks, and the wall swung open. Past the wall, there was a golf cart and a dirt path stretching endlessly down an unlit tunnel that reeked of seaweed. Brian tapped the same two bricks; the door swung shut, leaving us engulfed in darkness. We squeezed onto the golf cart, no easy feat for three very pregnant men. Luckily, Brian was small, and Enrico was skinny.

"Where does this go?" I had never imagined anything so elaborate.

Brian winked. 'It's about a mile long, and it ends at the lake. Daniel used this for protecting Monachee during the Last Gathering."

I had never heard that term, but I knew well enough what it was. It was just another name for mass incarceration, like the "Final Solution" in Nazi-occupied Europe.

Tyler said, "How was it used?"

Brian said, "It was the opposite of how we're using

it now. He'd drop off vanloads of Monachee at the lake, and we'd shuttle them in carts to the castle. That way, nobody figured out where y'all were going." The golf cart sputtered along before finally conking out.

Enrico cursed. "Pinche battery de mierda!" He fumbled in the glove box and lit a short candle.

Even angry, Enrico's face was handsome. He had a dark peach fuzz mustache sprouting on his upper lip.

Brian asked me, "What you looking at?"

I was caught. I blushed. "Enrico has a handsome face."

Brian strutted like a rooster. "He's mine, hands off."

Enrico turned sharply. "I ain't nobody's."

These two men were a couple! I was astonished. They looked like two hot cops. I hadn't ever realized cops could be gay, let alone in a couple.

Brian snapped back, "You're my bitch and you like it."

Enrico smiled. "Prove it."

Right there in the long, dark corridor, Brian unbuttoned his uniform and exposed an impressive chest covered with fur. His arms bulged with muscle that danced as he unbuttoned his tight polyester pants.

I thought this was just a show for our benefit, but Enrico stripped down, his thin hairless body a sharp contrast to his lover's hulking form. Enrico had a tiny penis, well below average. Even hard, it was too small for active sex. He didn't seem ashamed of it. His best asset was behind him. His ass was soft and round, forming an inverted heart shape of jiggling flesh.

Lonnie, the older orchardman, rolled his eyes and said, "Do we have time for this now?"

Brian's green eyes flashed. "Shut up! Watch the show. We're early."

It dawned on me that we were probably safer than we'd ever been in this hidden corridor. If it had a bathroom and a kitchen, I'd move in.

When Brian's pants fell, his dick sprang up and smacked his navel. It was pale, about the girth of a plump ballpark frank, but a little longer. It was perfectly shaped for a gay top to work his magic on a willing bottom. Enrico wriggled his ample buttocks in anticipation. Brian spit in his hand, rubbed it on his cock, then grabbed hold of Enrico's thighs. Enrico moaned in pure pleasure with no pain as his lover's familiar meat snaked inside him. I felt a pang of envy. If mine were less monstrous, the width of Brian's, I could have been a seedsman. Instead, I had a stack of coffee cans between my legs. I might as well be hung like Enrico. Nobody could ever take me, so I was forced to be an orchardman. Forced. That was what was wrong with this new society. The Monachee were stripped of choices, leaving only one or two depending on their anatomy. Our women had the least choice of all.

Brian ground his hips into Enrico's backside, spreading the massive butt cheeks so he could press further and deeper.

"Ay sí, papi!" Enrico's eyes fluttered while his tiny cock dribbled a thin clear stream of pre-ejaculate.

Brian pounded hard and fast. Without touching himself, Enrico came.

Brian kept fucking. "I make you come, don't I?"

Enrico nodded. Brian smacked him. "Say it!"

Short of breath, Enrico said, "You make me come."

These men had lives outside of the castle. They had private lives behind closed doors where they could commit capital crimes like buggery. And they were damn good at it.

Brian pulled out of Enrico. "Suck it. All the way."

Enrico obeyed. He was able to swallow the whole length easily. Again, I seethed with jealousy that Brian could get a full deep throat from his lover. Neither I nor Clyde had any chance of that happening. We were both hung ridiculously thick. Would I ever see him again? I feared he'd been arrested.

To take my mind off the envy, I focused on what the couple didn't have. Enrico would never be able to penetrate a man. If he somehow managed, it would feel like a thermometer, only shorter. Brian might benefit from another inch of girth. While he was able to enter his lover easily, he might not satisfy men who liked the stretch that a thicker man gives. And he was short.

Enrico made very little noise. Brian didn't cause him any pain, only pleasure. Enrico softly said, "Otra vez. Allí, próprio allí!"

Brian was hitting some spot that was exactly what Enrico needed. He shuddered; I recognized the anal orgasm. The involuntary squeezing put Brian over the edge.

"I'm coming, man, I'm coming!" He thrust his powerful hips until he was buried all the way. "Oh shit!" Brian grabbed his lover by the waist, holding himself inside as his balls pulsed. Enrico himself was coming a second time. When Brian withdrew, the two kissed passionately.

The candle went out suddenly; we were plunged into blackness.

The golf cart was completely dead.

Brian laughed, "It's only a half mile or less, don't worry. It's the last time we're ever gonna use it."

We walked in the inky blackness illuminated only by the relit candle until we saw moonlight reflecting off the lake in the distance. We quickened our pace, the taste of freedom hurrying us along.

14

DETAINED

When we finally emerged from the tunnel by Lake Michigan, I was astonished to see Clyde behind the wheel of a stolen ambulance. Daniel was still that terrible gray color, but he smiled weakly and held my hand.

"You made me the happiest man on Earth, Shep. I'm gonna pull through. You'll see. This baby will be beautiful. Three-fourths Monachee."

My mind struggled with the calculation, then, "Wait, you're half...?"

Daniel nodded. My mother fell in love with a Monachee man long before the plague. I was the result. I believe I'm the first Monachee male to be born of a woman in recorded history. I don't look Monachee up top, but below the waist, you must have seen some resemblance."

I thought about it. He was hung huge for a helmsman. Now, Castle St. John took on a new meaning. I had believed he was a helmsman running a sinister shadow operation. Instead, he was a rich Monachee running an underground railroad, selling babies to keep the operation going. Like any powerful man, he let the power corrupt him, but knowing he was of Monachee blood put the entire operation into perspective.

I wondered if Clyde knew. I came to his driver-side window.

"Did you know about all this?"

Clyde shook his head. "I was just a hired log of baloney. Everything was on a need-to-know basis, and all I really needed to know was how to prepare you for childbirth."

Tyler, Lonnie, and I clambered into the back of the ambulance. It was a straight shot down Archer Street to Midway Airport. At the gate to the private jetway, I heard a guard stop our ambulance.

"I'll need to see your paperwork. Who's back there?"

Clyde looked over his shoulder. "A very rich man who is very sick. If we don't get him to D.C. in the next two hours, he might die. So please consider the lawsuit waiting for you if you delay us."

After a long pause, the guard said, "I'm afraid I'm going to need to inspect first. Come with me."

The ambulance door opened, revealing Clyde and a muscular guard. The guard stepped back, pulling out a gun. I watched his eyes rove, landing on me.

"You, come with me!"

I obeyed. The guard licked his lips, examining my crotch. "You're a big one, aintcha?"

I remained quiet.

He turned to Clyde. "And you, are you smuggling a baby in your pants, or is that your cock?"

Clyde turned red. His lips curled into a snarl. "It's my dick, you son of a bitch."

The guard smacked Clyde hard with the gun. It left a welt on his cheek.

"I gotta have a head count before I return all you Monachee where you belong. Come on." He gestured with his gun towards the temporary trailer that served as his guard booth. I felt tears escaping. We were so close! How could I survive in another chicken coop after this? I probably wouldn't have to. They were gonna hang me for sure.

The trailer was lit by ugly fluorescent lights that recalled the hospital prison. They were the lamps of oppression.

"Okay, show me your cocks."

I turned to Clyde, baffled. He shrugged and unbuttoned his pants. Pulling his cock from his underwear, it fell, swaying from the sudden release.

The guard took a step back. "Holy fuck! Is that real?" Clyde's hog swung like a pendulum from thigh to thigh.

I followed suit. My darker cock tumbled to my knees. The guard put the gun in its holster, freeing both hands to grab our cocks. They fell from his grasp, heavy and far too thick for his short fingers to hold. He massaged his crotch. I noticed a thatch of hairs poking out the top of his cheap polyester shirt. Unsure what would happen, I unbuttoned it to reveal our captor's furry chest.

"Yeah, that's it." He pressed my head to his chest. "Suck them titties."

With both hands, he hauled my cock until it was trapped in the space between our bellies. He unzipped his khakis and pulled out his little cock, stroking it between his thumb and forefinger. A forest of pubic hair emerged from his fly. He kept one hand on his holster, protecting the gun.

"You!" He pointed his chin at Clyde. "Come here and suck on my other tit!"

Clyde obeyed.

The guard alternated between stroking himself with his free hand and fondling Clyde's monstrous meat. "How does a white boy get so big?" His words went unanswered.

I caught Clyde's eye and saw real fear.

The guard's breathing grew heavy. I knew that

sound. I'd heard it plenty of times before. He was close. In a bold move, I took the hand that covered his gun and put it on the side of my cock that was pinched between us. He rubbed vigorously. Again, I caught Clyde's eye. This time, he gave a knowing nod.

The guard said, "Oh fuck! You're both so fucking huge. Tell me how small I am."

I didn't hesitate. "That's a fucking nipple dick."

It worked. He was really turned on.

Clyde said, "You probably can't even get that thing in your wife's pussy."

The guard jacked himself furiously in tiny strokes. "I'm useless. Say it."

I said, "You're a useless piece of shit."

His eyes closed. "Oh, fuck, I'm gonna..."

In that moment, when he was over the precipice, I snatched his gun from the holster. He barely noticed as he dribbled a load on the front of his pants.

I stepped back, pointing the gun at the guard.

He laughed. "The safety's on."

He reached for the gun, but I pulled it quick and released the safety, training it on him again.

"Get down on the ground, asshole!"

The guard gave a gasp of fear.

"I mean it! Now!" I waved the gun, careful not to give him any opening to lunge for it.

Clyde swiftly kicked the guard's shin. "You heard him; get down on the fucking ground!"

The guard complied.

Clyde hauled his cock up and stuffed it into his underwear, zipping up. I realized I was still exposed. I couldn't zip up without risking the guard making a lunge for me. The last thing I wanted to do was shoot him. I'm not a murderer. And besides, the gunshot would bring reinforcements of some kind. That's when I noticed a half-dozen FlexiCuffs strapped to the guard's belt.

Clyde saw them, too. He snatched one and pulled it tight around the guard's wrist. He put another around his ankles, then hogtied the hands to the feet.

"Let's go!"

We ran back to the ambulance.

15

MILE HIGH CLUB

Back at the ambulance, there was no time for explanations. With red lights flashing, Clyde rolled over to a Grumman G-II. It was the kind of plane used by politicians and rock stars. Inside, there were enough chairs for everyone. Clyde and another custodian carried the gurney up the stairs. At one point, it rocked, and I thought Daniel and my unborn child would hit the tarmac. But they got him in unharmed.

With Daniel directing them, they collapsed a bench so there was room for the gurney.

Once Daniel was strapped in, we took off. I had been too busy to worry, but now I realized I had never flown and didn't know what was happening. The plane shook as it gathered speed. The engines grew louder. I thought something was about to explode, but then we left the ground. I could see Chicago laid out like a map. The cabin lights went out. I panicked until I saw the custodians leaning back in their chairs for a nap.

Clyde sat beside me and grinned. "Ever hear of the mile-high club?"

"What's that? Is it like the Elks Lodge?"

Clyde guffawed and then whispered in my ear. I blushed. He stood and shuffled to the back of the plane, closing himself into the bathroom. I stood and joined him. Everybody else was snoozing. The roar of the jet engines drowned out the sound of my footsteps. The bathroom was smaller than an outhouse. I didn't think I could fit in there with him, but it turned out that we could close the door completely once he shifted his enormous chunk of meat. Mine had nowhere to go but up, so it rested against my shoulder. The lotion was high quality, but it still burned a little. Pressing hard against the door, I was able to swivel my hips forward enough to allow Clyde entry. It was awkward, but once we were in position, he easily entered me. I was used to his forceful thrusts that separated my butt cheeks and dilated me, stretching my birth canal. My cock was at full attention, pressed hard against the door. Clyde sat down on the toilet seat, bringing me with him. I landed hard. I was pleasantly surprised when Clyde held my heavy meat in his hands and stroked it.

"You like that, babe?" He nibbled on my earlobe.

I nodded. "Why does it feel so good?"

Clyde smiled. "It might be the altitude. Makes everything swell more." To prove his point, Clyde flexed his cock inside me. It felt thicker than I remembered.

He tapped my leg, indicating that I should stand. Carrying the baby weight meant that I rose slowly. He ground and gyrated, stretching me in ways I never imagined. As he grew closer to orgasm, his thrusts built in intensity. Soon, I couldn't resist, and his hips pushed me hard against the door over and over. It sounded very loud from inside the restroom.

"Someone's gonna hear."

Clyde shrugged. "Nah. The jet engines are too loud. Oh shit. I'm close."

I prepared myself for his intense monster-like energy that came out just before orgasm. He roared.

"You like that! You like that! Just like that!"

Pleasure and pain were fighting a war inside me.

When he started fucking faster than a locomotive, the pain needed expression. I moaned at the top of my lungs. "Fuuuuuuuuuuck! Oh fuck. Oh fuck. Right there. Right there."

Clyde pounded a dozen times in five seconds, then held there and came inside me. Excess dribbled then flowed down my leg, pooling on the toilet floor.

Clyde stroked me hard. His hot breath warmed my earlobe. It sent me over the edge.

"Oh fuck! Clyde! I'm gonna come!"

I shot skyward, basting the two of us in white, buttery gravy. The whole bathroom looked like someone had put a firecracker in a tub of sour cream.

Clyde sat back and whistled. "That was the best yet."

I sat on his lap and kissed him. I felt him soften, then fall out.

I was still so turned on. I wanted more.

"Do it again!"

Clyde shook his head. "I'm getting a cramp. Let's get back to our seats before someone notices we're gone."

I wasn't having it. I put his soft cock inside me and ground my hips into his.

In ten minutes, he turned into a monster again. "Yeah! Shit! Oh, Jesus Christ. Oh, Jesus." He pounded the door with his fist. "Goddamn, I love you!" And then he came once more. He licked the length of my shaft to make it slippery, then wrapped both hands until his fingers nearly touched. He used his powerful arms to pleasure me in long strokes. In less than a minute, I was on the edge of orgasm.

"Clyde! I'm gonna come!"

"Do it, baby!"

I obeyed. The bathroom looked like it would never be clean. Our hair was matted, and our faces were soaked. Clyde wet a paper towel in the tiny sink and used it to wipe my face and neck.

He cleaned himself and wiped the floors. I took care of the mirror and the walls.

When we opened the bathroom door, the whole cabin cheered. Apparently, the jets couldn't drown out the sounds of true passion.

❧ 16 ❧

GEMELOS

We didn't dare stop a Gulfstream full of Monachee escapees in the US. We had enough gas to make it to Ciudad Acuña, just over the border from Del Rio, Texas. Stepping off the plane and planting my foot on Mexican soil, I got an uncanny sense of freedom. As Tyler and Lonnie stood beside me, we saw the locals point and speak. As far as Mexico was concerned, any Monachee was welcome on their soil, because it would help turn around the dwindling birth rate. The plague had passed over some villages, so some Mexicans were able to reproduce. But a massive influx of Monachee guaranteed that there would be many more generations to come.

Nonetheless, the citizens of Mexico weren't always happy to welcome pregnant men into their community. I could overhear the locals shouting out names like *"Higo relleno"* (Stuffed Fig) and *"Caballos a dos pies"* (Two-legged horses). I was grateful for that Spanish class back in high school. The names were a little hurtful, but it soon became apparent that they were really a form of endearment. The name-calling was filled with joyful laughter. Americans have big egos and seldom enjoy being ridiculed. But I could tell they were having fun with us, not at our expense.

It would take 60 minutes to refuel the jet, which was running on fumes when we landed. Tyler, Clyde, and I wandered into the airport lobby. Clyde had money, so he bought us each a *torta*, a delicious sandwich on a Mexican bun with bean spread, white cheese, avocado, tomato, lettuce, and the meat of your choice. I chose Milanesa, which turned out to be filled with a flattened breaded steak. It was as good if not better than anything I had eaten back home before the plague. They gave me a little clay jar filled with red sauce. I could see the chili seeds in the sauce. Spicy food doesn't agree with most Monachee, so I steered clear.

When we landed at Puerto Vallarta, the sleepy little village looked like it could slip into the sea at the slightest tremor. The downtown was stunning. Ever since Liz Taylor had filmed there, it had become somewhat of a tourist destination. The government was encouraging a "Mexican Riviera" along the Pacific coast. This meant that Puerto Vallarta was seeing millions of dollars in construction investments. The sky was filled with cranes.

Daniel approved of my relationship with Clyde. To bless it, he gave us about a hundred thousand dollars. It was small change for him, but we were able to buy our house with cash and still have enough money never to work again. We bought a house near Daniel, on the hill looking down over the village. It was an old Spanish-style place with arched doorways and beamed ceilings. The best part was the swimming pool in the backyard. When I got to my eighth month, moving around became a challenge. I had slipped a few times but never fell. In the swimming pool, gravity didn't matter. I was an okay swimmer, but during that last trimester, I became a champ.

Daniel's pregnancy was a few months behind mine. He was struggling to keep the child until the local hospital gave him a giant shot of estrogen. His nipples started leaking milk, and the color returned to his cheeks. He would keep getting those shots for the entire pregnancy. We just hoped it wouldn't hurt the child inside.

On a particularly hot, rainy day, I felt the stirrings of labor. Clyde was so excited to be a father that he nearly forgot my overnight bag in the rush to get me to the hospital. It had been years since a Monachee had been born in a hospital. I was born at home, and my kids were born in prison. I saw in Mexico the freedom that America had once promised. The American dream was in Mexico.

Thanks to Clyde's nightly poundings, my ass was loose and practically flapping in the wind when the placenta broke. Warm water that smelled like boiled hot dogs came out of me. This was nothing new. What was new was that it happened twice. The nurse said, "Gemelos." Twins. No wonder this pregnancy had gotten so difficult! Monachee never had twins. Ever. This was a rare birth.

The first baby left my colon and entered the rectum. The junction was tight, as Clyde rarely pushed past it during the exercises. The head pressed against my rectum walls. I blushed when the pressure aroused me, raising the hospital gown high above the table. The nurse and doctor were both very professional. They had seen many Monachee men get hard during labor. I wasn't so sure they were prepared for what came after.

As the baby left my colon and stretched my rectum to the limit, I thought of Clyde filling me up. As the little head crowned, everything reminded me of Clyde. The first baby pushed past my sphincter; the second one filled the junction. At last, the first child's shoulders pushed through, after which the torso, waist, and feet emerged in less than a minute. Even from my terrible vantage point, I could see that it was a boy. There's no mistaking a Monachee boy, as you can imagine.

My anal orgasms never subsided; they only grew in intensity. The second baby came much quicker. She was a girl. Daniel was in the waiting room, and I could hear him shout with joy at the news. He was their godfather, after all.

We named the boy Clyde Junior and the girl Juanita. We hired a nanny to look after them and help them absorb Spanish. Our money, invested in some pharmaceutical stocks, had multiplied several times over. We were rich even by American standards. In Mexico, we were extremely wealthy. A gourmet meal cost less than a dollar. And if we went to the restaurants frequented by the locals, the cost was half.

THE BET

About two months after the twins were born, a foot messenger came to our door, telling us that Daniel was in labor. The nanny hadn't arrived yet, so we left a hastily scrawled note explaining the situation and took the twins with us.

At the hospital, we could hear Daniel from the reception desk. We followed the howls until we got to the suite where the birth was taking place. The nurse blocked us from entering.

"I'm the father." Clyde had to entertain the twins while I went into Daniel's surgery theater.

Daniel held out his hand. "Come closer, Shep." I took his hand. He motioned me closer, then whispered in my ear, "You've made me so happy."

Then a contraction caused him to howl. He turned to me, his face screwed up in pain and anger. "You did this to me!"

"I know. You're welcome."

Daniel chuckled, then fainted. The team revived him with smelling salts. I could see right away what the problem was. The baby was coming out foot first. Back home, we used to push the baby back inside and rotate it until it was pointed the right way. These doctors didn't have much experience with Monachee birth. I used my best broken Spanish to tell them how to fix it.

The doctor answered me in English. "Put on some gloves first." In hospitals back home, they would never in a million years let me touch the baby. They were too worried about being sued.

I tucked my thumbs behind my fingers, making my fist as small as it could be. With the tips of my fingers, I pushed the baby's feet back into the rectum. Daniel was still out, so no cries of protest met my ears. With caution, I put first one, then both hands into the anal cavity. The umbilical cord was caught, so I unwrapped it from the child's neck, then turned him so his head was pointing towards Daniel's sphincter. Then, as was common in my family, I brought the baby out past the shoulders, letting Daniel's muscle contractions do the rest of the work. A steady trickle of blood came after. The doctors pushed me out of the way and inserted gauze into the gaping hole. The baby's cries woke Daniel from his swoon.

"Morphine! I want morphine!" The doctors obliged. Before Daniel drifted off, he extended a hand to me. "I carried the fruit. You planted the seed." Then his eyes glazed over and he nodded off.

I looked at the nurse. "Niño o niña?"

"Niña." I was the father of a second baby girl.

❧

WHENEVER THE NANNY TOOK THE TWINS OUT, THAT was our cue for sex. It got so that I almost got hard when the door closed! We had some modern patio furniture out by the pool. The chaise was my favorite sex bed.

One afternoon, the nanny took the twins to the local equivalent of a zoo. It was more of a house full of monkeys and another full of parrots, but it was good enough for babies.

The door closed, and my pants jumped. I got naked as fast as I could. I lay on the chaise, admiring Clyde as he stripped naked. His ass was bulbous and muscular. I found myself daydreaming about fucking him. I came awake when he slapped my face with the three-pound loaf of lunch meat.

Clyde grinned. "I want you to suck it if you can."

I said, "I'll tell you what. If I can suck you off, you'll let me have my way with your ass."

Clyde laughed. "I got nothing to worry about. So, it's a deal."

He put the thick pink baloney-colored meat just below my nose. I opened my mouth, and it landed on my lower lip. I didn't wait for him to get hard. I put the whole soft thing in my mouth and down my throat.

"That doesn't count. You have to let me come in your mouth."

I shrugged. As the meat grew swollen and heavy, it stretched my throat. I fought off a few involuntary gags. I realized I couldn't get any air. He was choking me with his fat cock. That excited me even more. I managed to pull back enough to take a few halting breaths of air before forcing the massive meat past my tonsils again.

Clyde was in heaven. No one had ever done this for him. "Fuck, Shepard, that feels good; wet and slippery."

He held my ears and fucked my face in extra-long strokes, giving me time to breathe between forward thrusts. I wondered why I had never tried this before. I remembered how it was punishable by death back in the New USA. In Mexico, anything goes.

Clyde was so excited by my blow job that he forgot the consequences of reaching orgasm. So when the orgasm monster appeared, and Clyde shuddered and roared, I felt my cock harden.

"I'm gonna--Oh fuck." He remembered, but it was too late. I buried my nose in his crotch and felt a warm river gush down my throat. Seeing Clyde's ecstatic face was reward enough, but we had a deal.

Clyde brought out the bag of Inca shortening. "How much do you think I'll need?"

"Here." I pulled him close and put my tongue on his hole. He shuddered. Soon my nose was buried in his ass, and his rectum was slippery with spit. Then I took a fingerful of Inca and put it inside. I spent time getting first two, then three, then four fingers into his tight hole. I thought he was going to back out, but instead, he started to moan. "Oh, Shep, that's, ooh, I can't believe how good it feels!"

I chuckled to myself. He had no idea what was coming next. To give him a preview, I worked my thumb in. I pushed gently, then hard, then gently until, at last, my knuckles crossed over. Now I could work more and more of my muscular arm into his virgin hole. I expected him to pass out or scream in pain, but he didn't. He moaned again.

"Shep, oh god, oh god. Why did I never do this?" He wiggled, trying to impale himself even more deeply.

"You like it?"

"Pull your hand out and put it back in."

I pulled and punched, letting my arm go deep.

"Aaaaah! Yes! Fuck I want you inside me."

Without losing a beat, I pulled my fist out and stuck my dick in him. He howled in pain. My dick's a lot bigger than my arm.

"Shall I stop?"

"Hell no! Fuck me!"

I didn't need much encouragement. It had been a long time. The sensation of being enclosed inside another man was a reminder of life before the plague.

Clyde's cries of pain dissolved into tears of joy. "Do it, knock me up."

I laughed. Clyde was not able to conceive. But then again, neither was Daniel. The thought of me making my lover pregnant was a massive turn-on.

"You want me to put a baby in you?"

Clyde nodded.

I picked up the pace, which caused a new round of cries to emit from Clyde's gaping mouth. But they were cries of pleasure.

"Do it, Shep. Put a bun in my oven."

The dirty talk put me over the edge.

"Clyde, I'm gonna come soon. You sure you want it up there?"

Clyde said, "Hell yes! Yes! Come in my belly."

My most vigorous thrust went deep, sending Clyde into paroxysms of pleasure. Then he had an anal orgasm. The vibrations on my cock were more than I could bear. I ground my hips into his backside. I ame.

"Ohhh! Oh, that feels so fucking good. I, oh, uh." Clyde ran out of words, which was unusual. He leaned forward, raising his backside in the air, allowing my cum to drift deeper in his belly. His body ejected my softening cock.

Clyde was delusional.

"If I stay here long enough, I'll get pregnant."

"You're not Monachee, Clyde. You can't."

But he stayed ass up, face down for half an hour. When he stood, a small trickle came out. He had absorbed the rest, I guess.

So, in a few weeks, when he threw up his breakfast, I rushed him to the hospital. The nurse did some blood tests and confirmed he was not only pregnant but also AB Negative, which was the Monachee blood type. It made sense. He was the thickest hung man I'd ever met. If he had length, I would have assumed he was Monachee. I guess he got the girth from the male side of the family and the length from the female side.

When the doctor gave the results, Clyde said, "I know. I'm part Monachee."

I was furious. How could he have never told me?

"You've known this all along?"

Clyde nodded.

"Why didn't you say anything?"

"In the new USA, I couldn't have said it, or I would have gotten locked up as an orchardman."

I saw his point but still had trouble shaking the anger. We were having another child.

Like with Daniel, Clyde's pregnancy didn't agree with him. He was ashen grey and had trouble balancing. I walked him into the Emergency Room. They gave him estrogen, and immediately his color returned. He walked back to the house without leaning on me once.

When the doctor gave the results, Clyde said, "I know I'm part Monachee."

❧ 18 ❧

THE MISSION

Daniel visited frequently with Isabela, his daughter. All three children were a year old now, and they had begun crawling, so we put them in a playpen together.

When Daniel stopped by, he was overjoyed at the news of Clyde's pregnancy.

"I'll have to rethink my plans."

"Plans?"

Daniel hesitated. "I'm leading a mission to bring back family members of the local Monachee. I had planned to have Clyde along, but he'll have to sit this one out."

I shuddered at the thought of returning to the ruins of that once-great nation.

"Shep, I need you along to point out your family members. You come from a royal bloodline so pure, even half Monachee can conceive. We need to bring them here where they're safe."

I would do anything to have my family back, but what if Daniel was planning to lock them up and force them to reproduce? I frowned.

"What is it?" Daniel put a hand on my shoulder; I pushed it off.

"Are you just going to lock us up again?"

Daniel laughed. "I was protecting you from a repressive government. All I ever wanted was for you to have children in peace."

"You mean you wanted us to have your children. We were all pregnant by you."

Daniel blushed. "I was on a real ego trip. I'm not now. I just want the Monachee to live in safety."

"Clyde, what do you think?"

Clyde held my hand. "You said you'd do anything to get your family back. You said it many times. Isn't this the chance you were waiting for?"

"But it's so dangerous. I have children to think of."

Clyde said, "Don't you want your kids to meet their grandma and grandpa?"

I nodded.

He continued. "I worked for Daniel for six years and never once did we get caught. His money is like a fortress. I'll look after the twins and Daniel's daughter. Bring your family home.

The next day, riding in the private jet, I felt the power of Daniel's money. Indeed, it was a protective force. It was also a powerful aphrodisiac.

While we refueled at the border, Daniel invited me to sit with him. "Shep, you're a father to Isabela. You made me a complete man when you got me pregnant. I'm feeling less than whole right now.

The silence begged to be broken. I said, "Does that mean you want me to fuck you again?

"I thought you'd never ask!"

We closed the cockpit door. I sat in a swiveling armchair that was perfect for sex. Daniel climbed onto the arms to get his ass high enough to find the top of my cock. He was much older than me, but his muscles were those of a young man. His ass was perfectly round with dimples on each cheek. I watched in fascination as sat down inch by inch. He winced when I turned the corner, but his smile returned immediately. At last, he rested in my lap. He put his feet on the floor so he could stand and sit. Despite his long strokes, I stayed buried inside him.

Daniel liked dirty talk. "Oh, Shep, you're so huge. You're so fertile. Put a baby in me." Daniel continued to slide up and down my pole, His cheeks parted to accommodate my girth. It looked like I could split him in two if I made the wrong move.

I began to gently thrust upwards to meet Daniel's descending ass. This brought him paroxysms of pleasure.

"Damn, Shep, I'm coming in my guts!" The rhythmic massaging of Daniel's spasms brought me to the edge.

"Daniel, I'm close."

"Do it; fill me up!"

I obliged. He climaxed at the same time. After, he stayed on my lap, kissing me. Eventually, I softened, When Daniel stood, I fell out of him.

When the jet was refueled and back in the air, Daniel approached me again. "Would you like more babies? I'm happy to oblige."

I was about to refuse when I thought of my twins and wished there were more siblings. Clyde could never make me pregnant - he was too thick and not long enough. Daniel had the Goldilocks cock - thick but not imposing, and very long. I got on my knees so Daniel could glide in and out of me freely. After Clyde, Daniel felt like a vacation. As he pushed into the fertile space in my gut, I shivered. It was a long time since I had been bred. I had been livestock, but now this was consensual. Daniel grabbed my meaty buttocks. "Shep, you're a beautiful man." He pinched and squeezed the base of my cock, arousing me. Soon his hand was stroking me in time to his pelvic thrusts. The overlapping sensations made me buck and sway.

To my surprise, I felt close to coming again, so soon after filling Daniel up.

"Daniel, if you keep rubbing me, I'll ruin your carpet."

Daniel rubbed even more vigorously. "Do it. I want to see you come."

Daniel nibbled on my earlobe and kissed my neck as he jacked me off. It happened. I shot the first load across the plane. It landed on the window opposite. Daniel said, "That's so hot."

As more of my cum soiled the seats and the carpet, Daniel picked up his pace.

"Oh fuck, I'm gonna..." He didn't need to say the last word, because I felt a sudden warmth in my belly. It was right where it needed to be. I was going to have another child by Daniel, I was sure.

AN INTIMATE REUNION

When we landed in D.C. at National, we were met by a sole customs agent. He saw my face and immediately asked, "Sir, what are you doing with a Monachee? They're federal property."

Daniel said calmly, "I found this one hiding out near the Mexican border. I'm bringing him back to Nixon Hospital, where he's from."

The agent looked at Daniel's passport. He didn't need one from me since I was just human livestock.

"Grant Horne, welcome back to the United States." I hadn't realized that Daniel had traveled under a different identity.

When we were out of earshot, he whispered, "I have many names and identities. When you have enough money, you can buy anything."

Grant Horne had a nice brownstone in Georgetown with a servant's entrance. He snuck me inside. On the wall was a map of the Potomac.

"You were at Nixon with your father. I believe your mother and sisters are at Jefferson Memorial."

"They told me my Pa went somewhere else."

Daniel nodded. "Yeah, that's what they would have said. He just went to the far end of the hospital."

"What's there?"

"When Monachee men hit middle age, they have a harder time conceiving. They use a test tube process there."

I didn't want to hear any more details. "And where's my brother?"

Daniel heaved a sigh. "So you're saying he wasn't at Nixon?"

I shook my head.

"Then he's probably at Richmond. That's a long, dangerous drive. We'll have to fly there after Jefferson."

Nixon Hospital was in Virginia. The taxi ride was long and expensive. 'Grant Horne' apparently had an arrangement just like Daniel's. He could bring his own seedsman into the facility and have private time with anyone he wished.

Past the sally port, we were met by a guard I recognized. I began to sweat until I realized that he'd seen so many faces every day; mine would never stand out. There was a hitch, though.

"Is your seedsman within the proper dimensions?"

Daniel/Grant hesitated. "He's a special request."

He dropped a hundred-dollar bill on the table out of range of any cameras. The guard picked it up.

"Right, then. Have you selected an Orchardman?"

Daniel said, "Boone Hendrix."

The guard laughed. "Boone? No way. He's been put to pasture."

I felt my blood boil inside me.

Daniel continued, nonplussed. "Boone Hendrix. He has royal blood, or so I'm told. I want a baby with provenance."

The guard chuckled and escorted us to the far wing of the hospital I'd never seen or even knew existed. The guard spoke to the custodian. They nodded.

"Take Room 618. He'll be along."

As I sat in the cold, clinical room, I felt all the

horror of captivity wash over me. We had once lived peacefully in the hills of Virginia. Now we were cattle.

Daniel said, "If your father sees you before they shut the door, he might give you away. Go in the bathroom and take a shower."

I did as I was told. The shower had seemed so nice when I was trapped here, but compared to the showers in our home in Mexico, it was like a dumpy motel room. I heard a commotion. Then I heard my Daddy's voice yelling.

"What kind of pervert are you? I'm nearly fifty years old!"

Daniel said something soft and soothing. The custodians who guarded my Pa were afraid to leave him with Daniel.

"Don't worry," Pa said, "I ain't gonna hurt him. Where's the seedsman?"

"In the shower, he'll be here in a minute. I heard the custodians shuffle off, and the door slammed.

"Come out now, Shepard."

My Pa said, "Shepard? That's my boy's name."

Dripping wet, I wrapped a towel around my waist and entered the room. I saw my father for the first time in over three years. He rushed towards me and held me in his arms. "What are you doing here?"

"I've come to bring you home. Well, to our new home in Mexico."

Pa smiled at Daniel. "You're the prick behind this, right?"

Daniel nodded. "I'm the prick."

We were locked in the room for the next hour. Daniel, ever the scientist, wanted to experiment.

"Boone, I got your boy pregnant. See, I'm half Monachee."

"You don't look it."

Daniel smiled. "Not upstairs, no, but downstairs..."

"I had twins with him, Pa. No seedsman, just him!" I was so anxious to please him.

Daniel continued. "I have babies all over the world now. I'm a stealth seedsman, if you will."

Pa nodded. "Why do I feel like there's a proposition at the end of this discussion?"

"Because there is. I will give you a choice. Let me impregnate you, or let Shepard do it."

As he said it, I felt all those longings I had felt for Dad before they died away in captivity. I blurted out, "Dad, let me put a baby in you."

Daniel added, "I'll watch and take notes."

Pa was not as ornery as he had been on the outside. He was used to being used. "If I let you watch my son do it to me, will you take me out of here?"

Daniel said, "I will do it regardless, but I, for one, would really like to see that.

Pa shifted in his jail scrubs, and I caught a glimpse of the outline of his massive cock. Like I said, nobody was bigger than me except my Pa.

Dad shucked his pants. There, leaning against his shin, was the biggest cock any of us had ever seen. My dad's cock. I wished I could let him fuck me, but I was probably carrying Daniel's child after our airplane encounter. So what? I had all the time in the world to let Pa do me, once we were safe. It was my turn to do him.

"I'm gonna knock you up, Pa. You better be ready for it."

Pa was out of practice. The skinny seedsmen were no match for my massive meat. He'd never taken me before.

With a generous helping of surgical jelly and some patience, I got the head inside. Pa pounded the bed.

"Fuck! Shep! When did you get so big?"

I kept pushing, it was time to turn left. I pushed at an angle, and slipped past Dad's junction, moving deeper toward the fertile place inside.

Again, Pa pounded the bed. "Owwww! It's too fucking big!"

"Not as big as you, Pa."

He was still soft. The pain was too much.

"Do you want me to stop?"

"Hell no! It's starting to feel good." Pa leaked a thin trickle of precum on the bed, signaling that the pain was dissolving into pleasure.

I was inexperienced, being my size and all, but with my pa, everything worked like it was supposed to. He was shaped right, like a full Monachee. I pushed deeper and deeper until I was at the place where babies grow. His guts wrapped tightly around me like a sausage casing. He started to vibrate.

Dad sighed. "I haven't felt one of these since I was with your grandpa." His stomach contracted over and over. His back formed a hump, then a bow. Over and over. And all that involuntary movement, coupled with the spasms inside him, felt like the best sex ever.

"Keep going, son. Put a baby in me." As he said those words, his softness swelled and lifted off the sheets, barely able to fight gravity because it was so heavy. Seeing Pa get hard sent me over the edge, to that place where climax was inevitable but not immediate.

"Oh, Pa! I'm gonna come!"

Pa looked back at me. "Do it, son. Come in me."

A few more strokes, and I was there. I released inside him. I missed my Pa so much, and it made the orgasm even sweeter. After a minute or two, Pa shot his load across the bed. The contractions subsided. He leaned back, twisting, and kissed me deeply, invading my mouth with his big tongue. I pushed back with my tongue. It was so good, I never wanted to withdraw, but time was ticking. I softened, and Pa pushed me out.

Daniel had stood by and watched. He was clearly aroused; there was no hiding what was in his trousers.

He took his clipboard and held it over his swollen pant leg. "That was beautiful."

I said, "How are you going to get us out of here?"

"Leave that to me." He stripped off his outer layer of clothes to reveal a doctor's scrubs. Now Boone, I want you to lie on this. He wheeled in a gurney from out in the hall. Pa climbed on it.

"In a few minutes, I'll need you to stay very still." He covered him with a sheet.

ℜ 20 ℜ

THE FEEDING TUBE

Daniel punched an alarm. A pair of custodians came rushing in.

Daniel said, "Cardiac arrest! We need to get him to an ambulance."

We were in a hospital, so it didn't make sense, but the custodians didn't question this man in doctor's scrubs. I helped Daniel wheel Pa out of the sally port to a waiting ambulance. Who should be in the driver's seat but Jedediah, the seedsman from the first night I met Daniel. He grinned at me. He was devastatingly handsome. I remembered how easily his relatively narrow cock had slid down my throat. I was faithful to Clyde, but if I was gonna cheat, it would be with him.

We raced down the expressway and across the Potomac to Grant Horne's house in Georgetown. On the bridge, Jed cut the sirens and lights. When we pulled up quietly to Grant/Daniel's service door, nobody noticed.

The four of us studied Daniel's map of the area familiarly known as DelMarVa. The Potomac took up most of the lower right portion of the map. Jefferson Memorial was in Chevy Chase. Richmond General was obviously in Richmond. It was too risky to drive an ambulance down 95 for 100 miles. First things first.

Leaving Daddy at Daniel's house to recover, we took another taxi to Chevy Chase. Of course 'Grant Horne' had connections with this hospital as well; they let us both in without even a question.

Daniel filled out some paperwork, and we were led to a grim room with three beds. At the foot of each bed were stirrups. This was where Monachee girl babies and "immaculates" were sired. They employed Seedsmen to produce fertile girls, and Helmsmen for sterile blood-related daughters. It never occurred to me that it took place in this factory-like setting. The thought of my Mama and two sisters being in this nightmare prison made me so angry that I nearly punched a hole in the wall.

Daniel shot me a sidelong glance. "Keep it together, Shep."

I blushed. As before, I hid in the bathroom to keep my family from blurting out their surprise at seeing me in front of the custodians. After fifteen minutes, custodians brought three Hendrix women into our suite.

"Where's your Seedsman?"

"He's in the shower."

"You know the two younger girls are pregnant, don't you? Both immaculates."

"How far along?"

"First trimester."

Daniel said, "We'll be gentle."

When the custodians left, I came out of hiding. My Ma wept. My two sisters came to my side and embraced me.

"Shepard, how did you get here? What are you doing here? This place is for women."

I answered their questions. With three women, it was going to be a challenge, but we were going to break them out of this place.

Daniel always had a plan. He pressed the alarm. Ma held my arm so tight I thought it would fall off.

Two custodians rushed into the room. "What is it?"

Daniel conked the biggest one over the head. The second one rushed me. I knocked him out. I took the uniform from the big guy, and Daniel took the other uniform.

When I put on my cap, you couldn't quite tell I was Monachee.

Daniel calmly marched to the hospital entrance where we had come in.

"These three women have a contagious parvovirus. It will likely kill their babies and the babies of anyone they associate with. I need to get them into isolation."

The guard blinked twice. "A parvo what?"

Daniel shook his head. "No time to explain. There's an ambulance waiting."

As if on cue, Jed pulled up, lights flashing.

The guard looked puzzled. "I ain't got no orders to let any of the hens out of the henhouse, sir."

Daniel produced an official-looking document on CDC stationery. As the guard read it, he blanched. "Can I just call Dr. Sweitzer to confirm this?"

Daniel said, "You go right ahead and call him, but I need to take these three ladies to isolation and final solution immediately."

"But them two are carrying immaculates. You can't do that."

Daniel pushed past and escorted Ma and the girls to the ambulance at a feverish pace. I looked back and saw the guard on the phone. He leaped to his feet.

"Hey!" But that was the last I heard because the siren roared to life, and I slammed the rear door shut. We used our lights and siren for a few minutes to get to a junction. Jed took a roundabout towards Baltimore and circled back on city streets and country roads until we at last pulled up to the service door in Georgetown.

Pa sobbed as he held Ma and his two daughters in his arms. He kissed their hair and squeezed.

Daniel interrupted the reunion. "I'm sorry, but that last jailbreak didn't go quite like I had planned. Grant Horne has been made. We need to go to a new safe house in Arlington."

The house was close to National Airport. It wasn't a nice place. The walls were papered with yellowed patterns. The whole place smelled like cigarette smoke. I sat on the fleabag sofa and wondered why Daniel had a dump like this.

He read my mind. "No one will look for us here, but we have a ticking clock. It's just a matter of hours before the Maryland State Police notifies all the airports. We need to be up in the air now."

My ma said she needed an hour to catch her breath and get her bearings. Daniel agreed.

There's a lot you can do in an hour. Jed followed me upstairs to a fleabag bedroom. I lay on the bed with my head hanging over the side. Jed put his knees beside my ears as he pushed his himself into my mouth, then my throat. He kept going until his crotch tickled my nostrils.

Like a locomotive drive, he moved back and forth in a slow, steady rhythm, gaining steam as my throat got slippery. Soon he was able to go all the way in and pull all but his cock head out before thrusting in again. I had a split second to catch my breath between strokes.

Jedediah beamed at me. "You're really talented, Shep. I mean it."

The compliment caused my loins to stir. Soon, I was at full attention. Jed held my hardness in his long, thin fingers, stroking me while making love to my mouth. If Clyde were here, filling my other hole, I would be in heaven. But he wasn't. I felt guilty, like I was cheating on him, but giving head is really not the same as what I do with Clyde. I shook the guilt and reveled in the pleasure of servicing Jed. He was in a heaven all his own. His eyelids fluttered. "I'm nearly there." He slowed down, but I knew we were due to depart soon, so I grabbed his meaty butt and pulled him to me fast and hard, in rapid thrusts. He threw his head back and moaned.

"I'm gonna come!" He tried to pull out so he could cover my face, but I was greedy. I pulled his crotch closer, savoring him as he came.

Jed was vigorously stroking me, and it felt good. He put his mouth over the top, licking and sucking until, at last, I gave him my cum in choking mouthfuls.

A loud yell came from downstairs. "Jed, Shep, we gotta go now!"

Jed brought Daniel, me, and my kin to National. When Grant Horne flashed his credentials, he was given carte blanche.

We drove the ambulance out onto the runway and boarded the plane. In the distance, we could see flashing lights and sirens. We wondered if they were for us. But we never found out.

We were given priority and cleared for takeoff. There was no telling if we would be treated as well when we landed.

21

THE CRAWLSPACE

Daniel explained his plan. "I told them we were landing at Richmond, but we're going to request emergency landing at Hanover County Municipal. You saw the flashing lights at National. They'll for sure be waiting in Richmond by now. Landing at Hanover will buy us a few hours, and keep us off the radar just long enough to get Junior out of the hospital. You're all to stay inside the plane except Shep.

My Pa protested. Let me go instead.

Daniel shook his head. "No offense, but you look too Monachee to pass."

"None taken."

Still in my custodian uniform, I disembarked. Daniel hired a limousine to take us to the hospital. He told the driver to wait.

When we passed the sally port, a guard was waiting. "Jefferson Howe, I believe I have an appointment." Daniel plopped down a new set of credentials.

The guard shook his head. "We had two jailbreaks tonight up in DC. We can't let no one in."

"But I have an appointment."

The guard looked at the roster. "I don't see you here."

Daniel said, "Oh, fuck it." He shot the guard with a tranquilizer dart, cuffed him, and took his keys.

Richmond made the other hospitals look like The Four Seasons. Every inch of the walls was covered with filth, and inmates jeered at us as we walked through the chicken coop.

"Do you see him?"

I shook my head. "I see an inmate I recognize from back home."

I called out to him. "Vardy. Vardy, it's me, Shep."

Vardy came close and squinted. "Shep Hendrix? Boone's boy?"

I nodded.

"Your brother is in here."

"Where is he?"

Vardy pointed out beyond the coop. "He's with a Helmsman getting stuffed. But they just called him a few minutes ago."

I could feel the walls closing in around me. I would be locked up again. Daniel's plan wasn't going to work.

Daniel said, "I'm the Helmsman, you're the Seedsman." I nodded, still doubtful but willing to go with any plan that might not end with me back in prison.

Daniel fumbled with the keys but found the one that would lead us to the conceiving wing. A custodian passed and glared at me. I smiled.

Daniel said, "First day. I'm just showing him the ropes."

The custodian frowned, "Who are you?"

"I'm from HQ." He held up the keys as reinforcement. "Say, you wouldn't happen to know what room Junior Hendrix is in?"

The custodian scratched his head. "I don't, but the clipboard is right there."

Daniel consulted the clipboard, then zigged and zagged past closed doors, all emitting moans and groans, until we got to room 369.

Daniel turned the key and opened the door. I was expecting to see a fat helmsman laboring to keep his tiny dick inside my brother's ass. Instead, it was just my brother, handcuffed to a table.

"Shep? Is that you?"

"Yeah. It's good to see you, Junior." A tear in the corner of his eye betrayed his nonchalance.

Junior waited while Daniel uncuffed him, then jumped to his feet, raced towards me, and nearly knocked me down with a bear hug. "Damn, Shep, you look scary in a custodian's outfit."

I searched around for Junior's clothes. They were folded neatly in a pile behind the bed. I hadn't seen Junior since he was a kid, barely eighteen. Now he was a man in every way. I felt a familiar stirring in my loins looking at Junior's cock, big enough to rival mine.

"Junior, you're huge. When did you grow up?"

Junior gestured to his cock. "Oh, this little thing?" He was getting hard too. It was weird to see my brother in a new light. In my family, love between adults was expressed in sexual union. Junior wouldn't be an exception. I was looking forward to a chance to feel him inside me. I'm sure he felt the same about me because he was lifting off, swelling, filling the room with his huge meat. He had me and Dad beat. He put on his clothes, hiding the prize.

Junior said, "Damn, Shep! I want you so bad!"

Daniel held a finger to his lips. There was a commotion outside the room. "Mr. Horne, we know you're in there! We're gonna count to ten, then we'll start shooting. Give yourself up."

I looked at Daniel in case he had this figured out, but the look of shock and fear on his face was all too real. He said, "I wish there were another exit."

Junior brightened. "There is! One of the Orchardmen got out through the ceiling. They haven't repaired it yet. That's why I was cuffed.

Daniel said, "I do believe there is a God."

We rolled the bed over to the hole in the ceiling. I boosted Junior, and Daniel boosted me. Then we both held onto his arms and pulled him into the crawlway. Gunfire erupted below us, but we crawled as fast as we could to a junction. We turned right, hit another junction, and turned left.

Junior said, "I think we're past the chicken coop. There should be a hole coming up that ends right at the sally port. Sure enough, we reached a giant hole in the concrete ceiling that looked down to where the guard lay dazed, cuffed to his chair. We dropped down silently and rushed out the sally port to freedom. The limousine came around in a wide arc.

The driver said, "They tried to arrest me. I got a wife and kids."

Daniel said, "Then come on! Let's get the hell out of here before they find you again."

22

THE END

Back on the plane, there were more tearful reunions. Before the cops could find us, we were airborne. We had enough fuel to make it to Mérida, flying out of radar range around the coast of Florida and across Northwest Cuba. The airport at Mérida was out of fuel, so we would have to wait in town for a few days waiting for the Pemex trucks to get there. The city is beautiful. There's a town square with a church built from the stones of a Mayan temple that had been there prior. You could still see Mayan glyphs on the stone walls. Doorways in Mérida were twice as tall as in the United States and ornately decorated. The houses were painted in faded mustard or bright tropical solid colors. Each night, the town square filled up with families and other city-dwellers to watch a show. One day, it was a clown from Mexico City. On another day, they did a traditional dance, balancing tequila glasses on wide-brimmed hats.

The hotel where we stayed had been a convent until only recently. Many of the employees were former nuns. I had never been sure how nuns regarded Monachee, especially us men, but these sisters made it clear that we were first and foremost human like everybody else.

We didn't have the plague; we were the solution. I never heard a whispered word of gossip between hotel employees. It was a relief to be seen as human. Vallartans were tolerant, but these nuns were more than that; they were respectful.

Bored in my hotel room, I watched the ceiling fan spin lazily, stirring the air just enough to provide relief. Then, a knock came at my door. It was Pa and Jedediah. Both of them had that look in their eyes that told me I was going to work for my supper.

Without a word, we stripped down, our proud manhoods jutting out in front of us. We came together. Pa turned his ass to me. "Just in case I ain't knocked up yet." Jed stood in front of me and Pa, stroking himself. Pa took my brother in his mouth. He choked, and the convulsions were just enough of a distraction for me to slip inside him from behind. When Pa felt it, he pounded the pillows, releasing a few feathers in the process. I worried he might bite down on my brother! We kept our voices down because it was a former monastery that sounded like an echo chamber. I spat on my exposed shaft and pushed in farther, reaching the junction where I had to turn left. Pa tore a pillow in two. Feathers everywhere, we laughed as I easily pushed into my Pa's deepest spot. It was easy for us both after that. Dad thrust his butt to meet my hips in rhythm to my strokes. Jed pulled out of Pa's mouth and pushed his hardness to my lips. I opened and took him all the way without gagging. I divided my attention between Jed and Pa. When I couldn't suck another minute, Jed gave it back to Pa, who greedily gobbled him down just in time to catch a mouthful of cum.

Quietly, with beads of sweat dripping from my forehead onto my Pa's back, I humped myself to climax. I fought off tears thinking about how long we'd been apart. It felt so good to be once more in each other's lives. I left my load deep inside. If he wasn't pregnant before, he certainly was now. Pa knew I was already with child, so he denied me the pleasure of congress with him. He was saving himself for Ma.

After two days, the Pemex tanker pulled into the tiny airport and replenished the jet fuel. We were airborne six hours later.

Landing at Puerto Vallarta, I wasn't prepared for the emotions I felt when I saw Clyde. My family knew nobody, but I had a lover. He frowned when he saw Jed. It was jealousy.

Jed gave a grin. "Shep didn't do it with me. I promise you."

Clyde shrugged. "Good, because I don't want to miss it when he does." I wasn't sure how to break the news that I was pregnant again with Daniel's child. Luckily, Daniel did it for me.

Clyde knew that he wasn't the right length and girth to impregnate me, which brought about feelings of jealousy and inferiority. He sulked around the house, begging off from family functions. One day, I'd had enough.

"Clyde, Daniel may have planted the seed, but you need to pave the road for the fruit to get to market."

His eyes brightened. "You're right." And pave the road we did.

Clyde unzipped his pants, letting them fall to his feet. His thickness rose slowly, reaching only 90 degrees. It was so heavy, it could scarcely fight gravity when it was fully engorged. He sat on a chair on the patio, his log waving in the wind. He pulled my ass to his lips, soaking it with spit. His tongue invaded my hole. It was a thick tongue, but it was nowhere near as wide as the invader to come.

When my butthole was slick with spit, I parted my cheeks and sat on Clyde's cock. Clyde moaned. He hadn't had sex since before I left for the US, so it was a welcome sensation. It had been a while for me, too. When we had sex regularly, I could take Clyde as easy as sitting in a saddle. But weeks had passed, and I wasn't used to him anymore. I silently cried as he pushed his way into me.

"Is that okay?"

I nodded.

"You sure?" Clyde was concerned because he was used to hearing me moan with pleasure. This pain was a temporary setback.

"Yeah, I'm sure." To emphasize my point, I sat down hard, taking all of Clyde inside me. My legs shook involuntarily as I stood then sat. The waves of pain turned into spasms of pleasure with each upstroke. The downstrokes gave me a complete feeling of fullness.

I said, "You're so huge."

Clyde flexed his kegel, getting harder, stretching my hole to its limits. Then, the spasms started. As my guts churned, they stroked and squeezed Clyde in a frantic rhythm.

"There it is." Clyde smiled, letting my internal contractions do all the work. I sat immobile in his lap, bringing Clyde close to coming with nothing but my twitching hole.

I was standing at full attention now. My cock leaned and throbbed against Clyde's strong shoulder. I was close myself. As the internal orgasm strengthened, Clyde leaned back and moaned with pleasure.

"Shep, I'm gonna come."

"Me too."

Without so much as a single stroke, I shot beyond Clyde's shoulder and onto the bed, the walls, and the ceiling.

"Unh. Oh. Mmmm." Clyde was past words because his balls were swollen with several weeks' worth of cum.

He climaxed, releasing his copious load. It was so powerful, I felt some of his seed move into my colo-uterine pocket. It occurred to me that Daniel's child might be sharing the womb with a twin now. Only time would tell what would come out.

EPILOGUE

Clyde's morning sickness abated when he started the course of estrogen. Seven months later, he gave birth to a premature boy, who lived on a ventilator for a month before he came home. We named him Tito. The twins fawned over their new baby brother. The house echoed with the sounds of toddlers running through the halls.

A couple of months later, I gave birth to another pair of twins, Juan Carlos and Emilia. Juan looked a lot like Daniel, but Emilia had Clyde's eyes. We were a strange family, with two daddies and no mother. But the beautiful house with a view of the blue Pacific was a great place to raise our children.

Daniel gave birth to a boy. We were breeding like cattle. My already pregnant sisters gave birth to two immaculate girls. My mother was pregnant by Daddy. There was no doubt it would be a girl. But Daddy was carrying two buns in his oven, one of them was mine. That was going to be one big boy!

Daniel never stopped running his Underground Railroad. He rescued Monachee from every state in the nation. I wasn't needed on these journeys, but sometimes, he borrowed Clyde to help usher Monachee to freedom. I couldn't sleep when Clyde was away, but it was for a just cause, so I cried myself to sleep at night with that in mind.

The Hendrix family included Daniel, Jedediah, and Clyde as honorary members. After so many years of being bred, we still never tired of sex. They didn't make rubbers in our size, so Daniel contacted a derelict condom factory in Tijuana and invested. They retooled their molds to accommodate the range of proportions. At first, they delivered in batches of a thousand. As more Monachee came to Mexico, the orders grew more frequent, until, at last, they began appearing on store shelves for a fraction of the price Daniel had been paying. They called them *Condones Gigantescos*. Daniel's knack for making money made him even richer. His investment paid off. The Monachee condom market in Mexico grew with each new group of refugees. Shares soared on the *Bolsa de Valores* until we were all swimming in money.

Once those condoms were available, we could plan our family. By the time the next generation got to child-bearing age, it was almost impossible to count the many possible couplings across and along generations. Monachee had always kept to themselves; this meant the siblings were often parents as well. With this brood, you never knew if you were your own grandpa!

The New USA crumbled. Autocracy spiraled out of control. In a bloodless coup d'etat, democracy was restored; the old regime was replaced by the Reformed Union of States. The hospitals closed. Monachee were free to return to their homes and live in peace. The re-formed States saw a decline in population, but the Monachee grew in numbers. The market for *Condones Gigantescos* grew worldwide as Monachee were invited to live freely and populate nations. The human race was ready to accept a change. Racial pride still festered in some nations, but they were doomed to wither and disappear. Cities in certain countries became hollow husks until, at last, they relented and allowed the new paradigm to take hold.

The Monachee would become the dominant subspecies, with traces of other genes living on in those rare children, like many of ours, who were conceived in a congress between a helmsman and a Monachee. Europe had once been the home of the Neanderthal, whose genes mingled with Homo Sapiens. It was time for another genetic shift.

ABOUT THE AUTHORS

Jean-Paul L. Garnier is the owner of Space Cowboy Books bookstore and publishing house, producer of *Simultaneous Times Podcast* (2023 Laureate Award Winner, BSFA, Ignyte, and British Fantasy Award Finalist), and editor of the SFPA's *Star*Line* magazine. He is also the deputy editor-in-chief of *Worlds of IF & Galaxy* magazines. In 2024 he won the Laureate Award for Best Editor. He has written many books of poetry and science fiction. https://spacecowboybooks.com/

Peter Schutes is the nom de plume of a prolific and acclaimed novelist. As Peter Schutes, he is the author of Adult Erotic Fiction such as The Slaves of Rome, Dark as a Dungeon, The Gospel of Priapus, and Panama Heat. He writes in the style of vintage pulp authors from the 1960s and 1970s. He lives in Los Angeles. https://peterschutes.com

Firehouse Lovers

The Fish

Five Erotic Tales

The Gospel of Priapus

Hercules and Lippos

Hobo Honey

Hoboes, Hustlers, and Outlaws

Hot Blue Collars

Hotshot

In Each Other's Arms

Like the Greeks Do

Little Shamus

Logger's Delight

Muscle Bottom

The Orchardman

Panama Heat

Satanic Seductions

Satan's Sissy Boy

The Slaves of Rome

Small Cockpits and Big Hangars

The Spotter

Steroid Steve

The Thigh Baby

Under the Boardwalk

Wee Dobbin

World's Biggest

***** Coming Soon *****

Tales of Two Daddies

More Tales of Two Daddies

Mowing and Blowing

Same-Sex: Gay SF Erotica